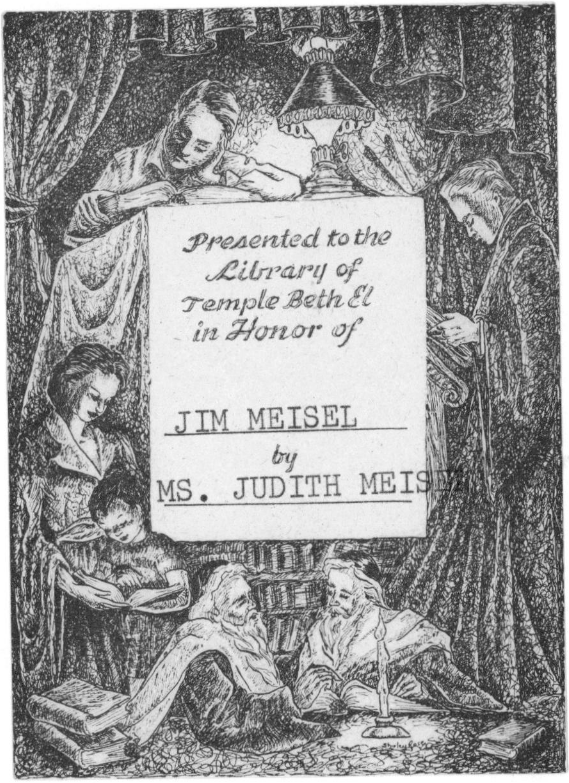
Presented to the
Library of
Temple Beth El
in Honor of
JIM MEISEL
by
MS. JUDITH MEIS

Cold Rain
on the Water

· Rose Blue ·

McGraw-Hill Book Company

*New York   St. Louis   San Francisco   Auckland   Bogotá   Düsseldorf
Johannesburg   London   Madrid   Mexico   Montreal   New Delhi
Panama   Paris   São Paulo   Singapore   Sydney   Tokyo   Toronto*

Library of Congress Cataloging in Publication Data

*Blue, Rose.   Cold rain on the water.
Summary: A Russian emigrant and his family face
challenges and problems in America.
[1. Emigration and immigration—Fiction.
2. Russian Americans—Fiction. 3. Family life—
Fiction] I. Title.
PZ7.B6248Co   [Fic]   78-23633
ISBN 0-07-006168-8*

1 2 3 4 5 6 7 8 9 MUMU 7 8 3 2 1 0 9

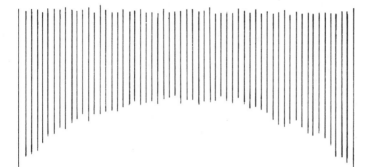

For Shoshana Kushner,
a super special person

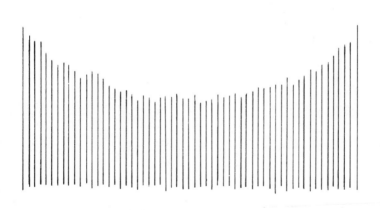

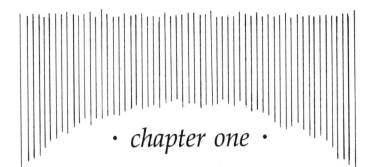

· *chapter one* ·

Alec leaned back and snapped his fingers to the beat. He picked up his cigarette and took a deep drag without lifting his head from the pillow. The stereo was cheap. He had bought it at Wild Willie's Electric Shock and assembled it himself. It had taken nights of careful work, but now the sound was high quality. You could hear every note, and the instrumental background on Native Son took concentration. "Cold Rain on the Water" was the group's latest, and it was a smash. Alec tapped his bare toes against the lightweight quilt as he grooved to the chorus of the vocal.

Cold rain on the water
Swelling the tide.
Chilling the morning.
Cold sadness inside.
We walk on the wet sand
Sea birds and me.
Cold rain on the water.
Cold rain on the sea.

Natasha burst into the room. The kid never bothered to knock. But Alec wouldn't act annoyed for anything. A guy didn't want to insult his little sister. Besides, being told to knock and wait till you were spoken to and stuff could cramp a kid's style. Alec knew that for sure. He wouldn't want to do it to Natasha. Not in this country anyway.

Natasha ran toward the bed, her dark hair flying.

"Alec, come quick. Look, we're on TV."

Now that the bedroom door was wide open Natasha was shouting above the six o'clock news and the stereo. Natasha tugged at his hand.

"Come on. We're on the news."

He sighed and doused his cigarette. He slid off the bed and shut the stereo. He loved American rock. It was the best thing about this country so far. But Natasha would give him no peace. She was one persistent kid. She grabbed his hand again.

"Okay, okay," he laughed. "I'm right with you."

Alec didn't bother slipping into his shoes. He just let himself be pulled into the living room.

Natasha plopped on the couch next to her parents. Grandpa sat on the soft, velvet easy chair with the loose pillow back. His gray hair framed his never-changing serious expression. Alec stretched out on the floor, his elbow on the rug, his chin in his hand. Some black guy was on.

"This is Lee Taylor," he was saying. "Bringing you this feature segment 'Freilach in Shtettle.' I spent a week in this charming, bustling Jewish community known as the Brighton Beach section of Brooklyn."

"He's talking about us," Mama said excitedly.

Alec yawned. The black guy spoke carefully. He seemed good natured and pleasant, even though he put the accents on the wrong syllables. The phrase *Freilach in Shtettle* wasn't part of his everyday small talk.

"There has been a new wave of immigration," the guy went on in his measured tones, "an influx of Russian Jews into this area. It's a good guess that they have chosen this area because of its closeness to the ocean. Our new Russian Jewish neighbors have always lived near the water. They probably feel at home here. In fact the area of Brighton Beach is now being called by many 'Odessa by the Sea.' Now let's take a look at some of our friends here."

The camera panned to quick shots of kids playing in the street, bustling restaurants, people gathered on street-corners talking. It sure looked like a *Freilach in Shtettle* scene. Cheerful, happy village. Joyous town. Alec shook his head silently. *Freilach*, bullshit. There was nothing heavy in this feature. Not a problem in sight. And, man, could Lee Taylor find problems if he looked past the end of his nose! The place was loaded with them.

"We'll be back tomorrow to fill you in on more of our series 'Freilach in Shtettle,'" Lee Taylor said.

"Isn't that something?" Mama said. "They're doing a whole TV news series on us."

"We must really be important." Natasha sounded impressed.

Everybody stayed glued to the color TV. The Steinoffs bought two luxuries when they came to this country. A used car and a cheap color TV. Frank Winter, the anchorman, went on delivering the news. "A new development in the president's energy crisis bill," he was saying. His voice had an even, soothing lilt to it. Alec shifted his weight, and let his mind drift back in time as Frank Winter's voice went on smoothly and evenly.

"People are leaving Russia just as they left Egypt in the days of the plague," Papa had said. "It's time we faced it. It may be now or never. Is it time to go?"

The eternal snow had been falling that night in Russia. Alec had looked at it fresh and white, drifting past the window in delicate patterns. He could watch the snow and dream. But Papa had called the family together to make a decision and the decision would be rough. Alec had to help make it. He wasn't a little child anymore. He couldn't avoid serious problems by looking at falling snow.

This night had been a long time coming. For many months the family had thought about leaving, flirted with the idea, talked about it, and then talked about something else. They knew that if they spent too much time talking about it the conversation would turn serious. So they pushed it away. But now, seated around the kitchen table, they were ready. Now the subject would not be changed. No more than things in Russia would be changed.

"We can't hide from it anymore," Mama had said. "It's like the Jews hiding from the fact that the Nazis were coming." Mama's voice had always been so cheery, so filled with life. Now it was sober and deadly serious. "It could happen here," she said chillingly. "And it could happen while the children are building their lives."

It was the market today, Alec had thought. He had gone shopping with his mother and Natasha. Natasha had wandered away and then came running to her mother. A boy about twelve was taunting her. "Dirty Jew," he yelled in a singsong voice. "Dirty Jew." Alec ran for him, but he ducked and disappeared in the crowd. Natasha clung to her mother. She wanted her mother to make it all well. But this wasn't something mother could kiss away. This wasn't something that would go away like a bruised knee. This was something that would spread and grow and get uglier. Alec had grown used to it. The ringing chorus of "Go, Jew, go" was everywhere. In the halls of the high school, in the streets, in the market. The three words had their own weird rhythm, like a song or a march refrain. But the chorus was growing too loud and life was growing too scary.

"The children are most important, Sonia," Papa had said. "Alec will be ready for college next year. You know how hard it is for a Jew to get into a good college here. And job opportunities are so much better in the United States."

"And your job, Isaac?" Mama had asked gently. "Your job is safe and secure here. Teaching jobs might be hard to find in America."

"Maybe," Papa had answered. "But if it's harder for us, then it's easier for the children. Each generation makes the next one better. If we go, we go for the children."

Mama had nodded silently and taken her husband's hand.

Suddenly the TV background music grew louder. It was a commercial. Alec felt as though he had been zapped back into another world like a passenger in some kind of crazy time machine. He looked at his grandfather. Alec could hear Grandpa's voice over the TV set. He could hear the voice just as it had sounded across the sea that snowy night.

"I will go anytime," Grandpa had said. "For me there is nothing here now. Shul is a dangerous place."

The old man was always the same, Alec thought. Back in Russia, here in America. When Grandma was alive. After she had died. Always, always, Grandpa was the same. Stiff and unchanging. Always cold, always stiff, always serious. Always holding himself in check, in control. Like father, like son, like grandson. Alec knew there was still a lot of that in himself even with the Americanizing, the loosening up, the new-found cool.

There was no problem in Grandpa's deciding to leave Russia. His only reason to leave was to go to a synagogue freely. There were government sanctions against going to synagogue in Russia and Grandpa was sick of hiding and sneaking around. His only interest in life was the practice of religion, and he didn't much care where he practiced it. If you could go to temple in America, then that's where Grandpa wanted to be.

"It's best to go where the children can learn their religion in peace," Grandpa had said that night. "Children must learn to do what's right."

Alec looked at his grandfather, still sitting stiffly against the softness of the velvet-cushioned back pillow, still sitting in the same position.

"Children must learn to do what's right." Doing right. That was the slogan of Grandpa's life. He always did what was right. He had worked, supported the family, studied his religion, taken care of the needs of his children. Alec knew he loved his grandchildren, but Alec didn't know how he knew it. There was never any Grandpa to lift Alec up in the air, hold him on his lap, bounce him on his knee. Here there were loving parents and jolly, warm, hugging grandparents all over the TV screen. Grandpa was a far cry from the Waltons.

The TV background faded out again. Alec looked at the colors on the screen and saw the white snow falling past it. The snow that fell past the window that winter night in Russia.

"We're talking about what's best for the children," Papa had said. "Now we must ask the children how they feel. This is a family decision." Papa looked from Natasha to Alec.

"I've heard they have good shows on color TV every night, in America," Natasha responded cheerfully. "And all kinds of ice cream. Is that right?"

"I think so," Mama laughed.

"Then let's go," Natasha said firmly. "I think I'll like it there."

Papa's eyes held Alec's. "And you, son?" he asked quietly. Alec knew what his father was thinking. He knew his father's thoughts a lot of the time. Their minds worked in much the same way. Alec knew that it was easier for Natasha to say "Let's go." It was easier to make decisions when you were nine. But sixteen was a lot rougher.

Alec had his friends and his school. He was used to the school. In Russia it was strict and rigid. There were rules and you obeyed them. You listened to your parents, to the law authorities, to your teachers. But you didn't have to think too much. There was a kind of security in being told what to do. Like a clear road map when you went on a trip.

There were the same friends from childhood. There was

Boris who had come over every day since kindergarten. There was Ivan who was around all the time laughing and eating everything in sight. And there was Edna. She was his girl friend. She was Jewish. She was suitable. He took her skating, to the movies, to concerts. There was no sex, though. Not that early. Later the friendship would lead to serious dating, then marriage. Alec knew what to expect in Russia. He knew what to expect from Boris, Ivan, and Edna. The human temperature was always the same. The cold weather never bothered Alec, the cold inside the house or out. But this night Alec shivered. This night Alec felt cold and icy deep inside.

There was a lot to give up when you left your home of sixteen years. Far more for his parents to leave behind. Far more for a man to leave his work behind.

He knew English wouldn't be too much of a problem for his family. Grandpa did nothing but read and study all the time. He knew Hebrew, English, French, and probably every language but Sanskrit. Papa was a teacher and a serious student too. And Grandpa was always teaching Alec. It seemed that teaching was about the only way Grandpa knew to relate to kids. Alec came from a long line of scholars. Mama had studied languages in college too. She knew English quite well. And Natasha would pick it up in no time. The kid learned fast. She was really smart.

Alec sat frowning, weighing. He saw the scale in the market tipping this way and that. Then he saw Natasha running crying in the market. He heard the boy yelling "Dirty Jew." He heard the chorus "Go, Jew, go. Go, Jew, go. Go, Jew, go." It wouldn't stop. It would grow louder and louder. It would get a lot worse before it got better. If it ever did get better.

Alec looked at his father, then at his mother.

"It's hard to leave," he said softly. "But if life can be better, then I guess we have to try."

"Try is all we can do," Papa said.

Mama squeezed Papa's hand tightly. "I think we must try," she said. "For the children."

Papa nodded. "I agree," he said firmly. "Then it's settled. We leave."

After the decision to leave was made things moved fast. Normally the red tape was endless. The approval to leave took ages if you ever got it. Then Hebrew organizations helped pave the way out. Everyone who left took the same route. Russia to Vienna to Rome to America. Each step of the journey was a mile.

But Grandpa cut the red tape. He knew who to deal with. There were secret conferences over tea glasses with a rabbi. Not the rabbi you saw in synagogue. Not the rabbi you saw in the street. But an old, white-haired, bearded chief rabbi. Grandpa never told Alec what was said, or how he knew the rabbi, or who the rabbi knew. But later, looking back on it, Alec thought it was like an underground James Bond with glasses of tea instead of very dry martinis.

But Grandpa's talks led to quick visas. Quick one-way tickets out of Russia. The Russia–Vienna–Rome–New York route was speeded up, thanks to Grandpa and the mysterious rabbi. But everything was arranged for the immigrants like a no-questions-asked charter flight.

Alec remembered the airport scene in New York. He remembered it clearly because the first step on American ground brought sights and sounds of trouble. He remembered the confused people, unable to speak English, unable to understand the customs officers.

Mama kept running the fingers of her left hand through

her hair trying to hide her rings as she had done back in Russia. There were many stories of jewelry being taken from people at the Russian border. Nobody here bothered Mama. But many families did have problems.

There was the family who tried to hide some kosher meat.

"Do you have any fruit or meat?" the customs officer asked. Alec figured they asked because they didn't want contaminated food entering the country. Still, the poor family was scared and tried to hide the meat.

"What have you people got there?" the customs officer asked angrily. "What are you trying to hide? You're making our jobs harder."

Grandpa had stepped in, translated, explained. The Steinoffs did what they could, but the airport was a mess. People wandering around carrying bundles, bedding, teapots. Heavy burdens seen and heavy burdens inside that you couldn't see. You could see it in their faces though as they wandered around looking for relatives. Sometimes there were reunions, family members finding each other, hugs and happy tears and clinging, clinging.

Alec remembered the people with tattoos. They wandered around searching for other people with tattoos on their arms. The numbers of the Nazi concentration camps. They wanted to find each other, those people who had been in the camps. They wanted to share their special sorrows. The people who had been persecuted in one place and time. Nazi-occupied countries, then Russia. Alec thought of those airport tattoos whenever he saw one in America. And each time he saw one, he thought—double trouble, now triple trouble.

At last the airport scene calmed down a little. A Hebrew organization on this side of the ocean helped get the new immigrants settled. They put the Steinoffs up in a motel near the airport for one night. The next day the Steinoffs looked at some apartments. They learned that many Russian Jews came to Brighton Beach. It was near the water, like home. Alec felt a little better about that. He had always loved the sea. The Steinoffs saw a few apartments and then settled on one. It was in an old apartment house, old but clean. The rooms were big. There were two bedrooms. Alec would share the second bedroom with his grandfather, and Natasha could sleep in an alcove off the living room on a couch that opened into a bed. The journey was ended. Now the Steinoffs had a place to live. Now the family had a new home.

The TV sound rose sharply once more. Another commercial was coming, even louder than the others. Alec's eyes focused slowly on the screen as though he had just awakened to the morning light. A babble of voices surrounded him. The family was talking above the TV sound. They did a lot of that in this country, Alec thought. In Russia you sat around and talked. But here TV was like a narcotic. Not much different from pot. Except most everyone seemed to get hooked. Alec didn't get hooked on American television though. For himself, he dug music. In Russia he had listened to classical and Russian folk music. But the latest American rock sound had not yet arrived there.

Alec looked at Natasha. She was glued to the set watching the anchorman, happy as a clam. Happy, like the kid was in her right mind. Natasha had just turned ten and Alec had turned seventeen last month. But the seven years might as well have been a hundred. Alec was going on to being an old man, heading to Grandpa by way of Papa.

Frank Winter was talking. "Be sure to tune in tomorrow," he said. "We'll have more on our feature series from Lee Taylor."

"Isn't that interesting?" Mama commented. "We'll have to watch the news on this station tomorrow."

"I'll watch," Papa agreed. "But I wonder if we'll learn anything we don't already know."

"I don't think so," Grandpa said. "Too much is learned from television here anyhow. Too little is learned from books." He turned to Alec. "Even you don't read so much anymore, Alec. You don't watch as much television as many people here do. Still you don't read as much anymore. You should look at the books on our shelves, Alec. You should visit the library more regularly."

"You're right, Grandpa," Alec responded respectfully. "I finished some books last week. I'll bring them back tomorrow and get some new ones."

The old ways, Alec thought. New country. Old ways. Respect your elders. Not every kid would answer his grandfather the way Alec did. But not every kid had Alec's grandfather. Or Alec's father. It was deep in the family. Deep in tradition. Deep in the genes. You didn't lose it in a transatlantic plane ride.

"We learn from books," Papa observed, "and we learn from experience. It's hard to learn. And one of the things we learn is that life is hard."

Alec looked at his father. Lately each time Alec looked at his father he felt like crying. The man always looked so down. He appeared so much older than he had in Russia. It was hard to believe that only months had passed since the plane that brought them touched down at Kennedy Airport. Yet for a man with no job, a man with no future in sight, the months must seem like years.

"Tell me, Alec," Papa said, "are classes starting soon?"

"I got the college catalog last week," Alec replied. "Freshman registration isn't for a few weeks. Classes don't start for awhile."

"School starts late here," Papa said.

"I guess so, Papa."

Alec pressed his hand down hard on the carpet. In Russia Papa wouldn't have to ask when classes started. He would know the school calendar for college, for high school, for everything. In Russia Papa would be teaching by now. In Russia Papa would have a job.

Alec would have to do well in college. He wasn't sure what he would major in yet, but he would have to study hard. Get high marks. He would have to find a part-time job too. He had to help the family. He had to make good. His folks had given up so much to come here for their kids. He couldn't let them down.

Mama got up. She shut off the six o'clock news. She leaned down and rumpled Alec's hair. "My son, the college man," she laughed. "My big, strong, smart, handsome son. He's really growing up. Come on, Alec. Get up. I want to see how you've grown." She tugged his hand and teased. "Come on. Get up. You'll wear a hole in the carpet."

Alec smiled. He stood up, holding his mother's hand. She turned her back to him and put her hand above her head, her rings catching the light.

"One head, one and a half heads. You're one and a half heads taller than your mother now. The men in my family grow tall."

She leaned down and kissed Papa's hair.

"Look how lucky I am," she boasted. "I have two big handsome men. Two tall, sandy-haired, blue-eyed men.

And me with black hair and dark eyes. There's an old saying that you know who the mother is but you can never be sure about the father. That's not true in this family. All you have to do is look at the father." She whirled around swinging her skirt. She patted Grandpa's gray hair. "And my other handsome blue-eyed man."

Grandpa smiled. Mama was the only one who could make Grandpa smile. Mama could make anybody smile. She was trying hard now. It was rough on her. Working, trying to lift Papa's spirits. She was looking kind of worn lately. But she was trying. Trying to lighten the evening.

In Russia Mama always brightened the nights. The nights there were colder, longer, darker, yet here they were so much harder for Mama to light.

Grandpa moved forward in the chair, where he was sitting. Alec watched him hold the arms of the velvet chair as he lifted himself slowly and studied his watch. Alec knew just what Grandpa would do and say. It was the same every single night. "I must go to shul now," he said. "It's almost time for the evening service."

Soon Alec could be alone in the room he shared with his grandfather. He could blot out everything and everyone and listen to his music.

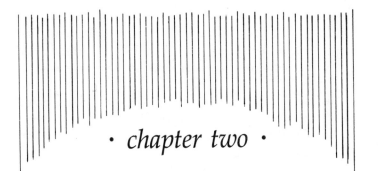

· *chapter two* ·

It was a quarter past six when Alec left the house the next night.
The family sat gathered around the TV set watching the six
o'clock news.

"Alec," Natasha reminded her brother as he stood up,
"you can't go out now. Lee Taylor is coming on soon.
You'll miss him."

Alec bent down and kissed his sister's cheek. "Well,
little one," he laughed, "you tell me all about it tomorrow."

"I'll forget," Natasha answered seriously.

"Well, you can always take notes."

"Have fun, Alec," Mama said. "We'll let you know if
tonight's feature is interesting."

Alec flung his denim jacket over one shoulder the way

the American kids did it. He had studied the gesture carefully, and now he had it down pat. Big deal, he thought as he closed the door behind him. He would miss Lee Taylor's phony sugar-coated series. That sure was no great loss.

Alec ran down the apartment house steps. The Steinoffs lived three flights up. Alec never bothered with elevators. He had left a little early but tonight was teen group night at the Beachside Y. The teen group met Tuesdays and Thursdays. Leonard Manfeld was the social worker who ran the group. Leonard was a young guy. He was about twenty-three, and had been in the country for a few years.

Alec enjoyed the Y. It would be nice if the group met more often. But they let the kids use the gym during the week even when Leonard wasn't there. Alec liked to work out as often as he could. The high school in Russia put a lot more stress on athletics than Hayes High did here. The American kids weren't really into building up their bodies.

Everyone had spent most of the summer hanging around the beach. That was where the whole crowd met. Like it was a social club. Now it was early fall, and the area around the beach grew more chilly than other parts of New York. The Russian kids were used to it but the American kids always seemed colder. Now the crowd would begin moving indoors. Now the Y would be the main hangout.

Alec stood in front of the house for a minute. It was a nice night. He decided to walk along the boardwalk. He was taking the long way to Beachside Y. But Alec liked to walk and he liked to look at the ocean.

He walked quietly up the boardwalk ramp, inhaling the salt air that drifted in with the ocean breeze. He jogged awhile and then he stopped and held onto the railing. He felt like watching the sun moving lower toward the ocean, its rays glinting like bouncing gold coins on the blue water. The sights and sounds of the beach had helped Alec when he had first come here. The sunset over the water had helped ease the aching homesick feeling.

Now the yearning for home came less frequently. Alec still thought about Boris sometimes. Boris had always been at his side every school day. He thought of Ivan once in a while when he saw the kids stuffing their faces at Quick Grill. There were cafeterias in Russia but no fast-food places. Ivan would never stop eating long enough to come up for air if you took him to Quick Grill. And once in awhile Alec thought of Edna. But the sweet, gentle face was beginning to fade from his mind. He would picture Edna but see Felicia, his girl friend here, laughing, moving, tossing her hair. It was like an action scene blotting out stills on a movie screen.

He felt pretty comfortable with the kids here now. Part of the crowd was Russian, part American, but everybody was Jewish. They weren't the same as friends you shared your childhood with. They couldn't be the same as friends you shared your entire life with. But this was another place and another time. Things and people were different, and in many ways so was Alec.

It wasn't hard to learn English. He had known English for years. But it did take a while to learn to speak American. He caught on pretty quickly though and now he often thought in teen-age American slang. There was still something of a mix in Alec though. Some Russian, some American, like the group at Beachside.

He took one last look at the setting sun and then ran along the boardwalk and down the beach block to the Y. It was still early and hardly anyone had gotten there yet. Alec looked around the teen lounge area. One lone dark-haired boy sat glued to the TV set. The set was in a tiny room off the hall. Nobody came to the Y to watch TV. You could do that at home.

"Hi," Alec greeted the kid. "You new here?"

"I am called Leon," the kid answered in labored English.

"*Zdravsteruyte*," Alec said. "Hi."

"No," Leon corrected him. "No Russian. I want English. What are you called?"

"Call me Al," Alec said. "Everybody does."

It was true. Everybody called him Al. One of the first things Alec said when he spoke to new kids here was "Call me Al." Alec could dig the kid now. It was only natural. You wanted to fit in. You wanted to become American as quickly as possible. You wanted to take a crash course in Americanese. Alec had done it himself early on. Sat in front of the TV set for hours just to study American ways and dress.

"You'll like the group," Alec told Leon. "There are American kids and Russian kids. Everybody's Jewish."

"I am not Jewish," Leon said.

"Oh," Alec said. He was surprised.

He didn't know there were any Russian families in Brighton who weren't Jewish. "Well, that's okay. You'll like it here anyway."

"I was Jewish," Leon said. "I was Jewish in Russia. Now no more. Now I am American."

Wow, Alec thought. That was heavy. Not everybody reacted the same way when they came here. Not everybody wanted to be a quick-change artist and become American. Some kids were very clannish. They spoke Russian in small groups. Resisted American ways. Avoided making American-born friends. But the way Alec saw it, if you wanted to make good in this country you had to be part of it. Still, Leon was going too far. He had come here to escape the anti-Semitism in Russia, and now he was trying to escape from himself. But maybe in time the new kid would adjust. Maybe it would get easier. Just maybe. Alec looked at the kid. He was still gazing at the TV set.

"Later." Alec waved.

He left the TV room and walked down the hall.

"Al," Leonard called. "How's it going?"

"Fine, Leonard. What's up?"

"Come on in and we'll show you."

Alec walked into the small room. Leonard and his group were sitting around a table. Misha was there and Betty and some other kids. Some were American and some were Russian but they were Leonard's group. They were the Soviet Activist Group. They sat, talked, played chess, but mostly they did work for the activist groups here and the underground network in Russia. All the kids at the Y liked Leonard just fine whether or not they were interested in his activist group. He was so busy with this work that he never paid too much attention to what the teen group was doing. That was a lot better than having a nosy social worker snooping around you all the time.

Leonard moved his glasses back onto his curly red hair.

"Sit down, Al," he said.

Alec didn't really feel like sitting down. He wanted to do something athletic, and there was so much good stuff at the Y. But he couldn't say no. He had too much respect for Leonard and his group. Leonard had led the Free Maritza Gellman Campaign here last spring. Maritza Gellman was in a Russian prison charged with anti-Soviet activities. Leonard had written the literature and gotten hold of a printing press somewhere. He and his group were something else.

Alec pulled up a chair. "What's happening?" he asked.

"See this list?" Misha nodded toward some sheets of paper clipped together. Alec picked them up.

"Yeah. What is it?"

"Names and addresses," Betty spoke up mysteriously. "Names and addresses of mothers and children."

"I don't get it," Alec said.

"Tonight is born-in-September night. This is a list of children still behind the iron curtain. They are the children of Soviet activists. Their fathers or mothers are jailed or dead or who knows where."

"How did you get the list?" Alec asked.

"We have our ways," Betty replied smugly. "Anyway, these children were born in September. We're sending birthday cards to them to show that we haven't forgotten. That we haven't forgotten them or their parents."

"That's a great idea," Alec said.

"Sure is," Leonard agreed. He moved his glasses back in place and pulled a sheet of paper from the clip. "Here's part of the list, a pen, and some cards. Dig in and start helping."

"Sure, Leonard," Alec said.

He picked up the sheet and pen and wrote quickly. He didn't talk. He just concentrated on his share of the work. Leonard and his group were doing terrific things. Alec was glad to help out. But he wanted to finish so he could get up and move around a little. He had the cards written out and addressed in about twenty minutes. He stood up.

"Okay, Leonard," he said, "I'm done. I wrote a little message on every card too."

"Far out," Leonard said. "Thanks. Maybe you can drop by later or on Thursday. We'll still be working on the cards at our next session."

"Sure," Alec said. "Glad to."

Alec waved and left the room. He walked down the hall of the Y. There were signs on every door, some open, some closed. Every sign told of a different service provided by the Y. The funds given by the federal government, the Jewish charities, and the Hebrew organizations were spread every which way. There were old people's groups, language classes, and job counseling services. Anyone walking through these halls would think of the Y as one big "Do everything for me center." Anyone just off the plane from Russia might really take it seriously. Why not? In Russia everything was planned for you, scheduled for you, done for you. But here the signs on the doors pointed to a dream. Here you made it yourself. Here, on this side of the sea, it was different.

The sound of the ball against the table drew Alec into the Ping-Pong area. Ernst and Mike were playing. Alec stopped and watched. They were both of medium height, Ernst dark-complexioned and Mike fair. They lived in the same apartment house and had become good friends. Ernst had come here about a year ago and Mike had helped teach him the ways of the new world.

"Hi, Al," Ernst greeted him. "Did you hear?"

"Hear what?"

"It happened today at Hayes," Mike said. "Ernst was there."

The two guys were so good they finished the last point while they were talking.

"Your game, Ernst." Mike put the paddle down.

"Want to volley with the winner?" Ernst asked.

"Sure do," Alec said. He was itching to move. He picked up the paddle and served.

"What happened at Hayes?" he asked Ernst. "Isn't summer school over?"

Ernst was going to school this summer to catch up on English. Alec had no trouble graduating way ahead of the class and didn't need any extra time. His guidance counselors had arranged for his college applications and entrance exams in the spring.

"This is the last week for special make-up classes," Ernst said. "Anyway, this Russian kid was in the bathroom today. His name is Yudi. I don't know him. But it seems this Puerto Rican kid came into the bathroom. The two of them had words and the Russian kid got knifed."

Alec missed the shot. "Knifed!" he exclaimed shakily. "God almighty."

"It wasn't that bad, Al," Ernst said. "It was just a pen knife or something. Just a flesh wound in the shoulder. A teacher heard the racket and came into the bathroom. But the Spanish kid ran out. The teacher ran to see about Yudi, and he didn't get a look at the guy who did it. A lot of the new Russian kids aren't used to seeing anybody who's Spanish. So Yudi couldn't identify the kid who did it."

Alec nodded. "People have to get used to each other. But that's terrible."

"Yeah," Ernst said. "Some of the tougher Russian kids are mad. All the Russian gangs and the Puerto Rican gangs need is an excuse to go after one another."

"That's right," Mike agreed. "The way I hear it there's going to be trouble."

Alec served again, harder than before. Trouble. More trouble. As though we didn't have enough of that already, he thought. Alec remembered hearing that immigrants had come from Europe years ago thinking that the streets of America were paved with gold. Alec figured it would be pretty sad if anyone believed it these days. These days there was more blood than gold on the streets.

"If there really might be trouble," Alec said, "maybe we can head it off. Maybe Leonard can help out. He's smart."

Ernst shook his head. "I doubt it. Leonard's a good guy but he's really into his Soviet Activist Group. He wouldn't have time for much else."

"Besides," Mike said, "I doubt there's much he could do. There's a lot going down. It's not simple. The Spanish figure they were here first. They think they staked out the area. And now the Russians are coming. Cutting in on their neighborhoods and their action."

"What action?" Alec asked. "Everybody's having such a rough time keeping out of the poorhouse I don't see what there is to fight over."

"What little there is," Ernst said, "is what there is to fight over. They figure we're competing for jobs for one thing. Besides that, there's the drug pushing and stolen goods action and stuff. You know some of our kids aren't so kosher either."

"Yeah, some of them have been in trouble with the law already. It's the difference between the way we were raised in Russia and how things are here," Alec reflected. "There's so much more freedom in the schools and with the authorities."

"Yeah," Ernst repeated. "It's rough to handle sometimes. The kids figure they can get away with anything here. Nobody throws you out of school or locks you up and throws away the key. Some kids are just not afraid of anything here."

"Like Morris," Alec said. He laughed. Even in the midst of all the heavy problems there was something funny about Morris. He went around pushing soft drugs, and he didn't care if the noonday sun was shining or the cops were ten feet away. When the other kids asked Morris why he wasn't more careful he just shrugged his shoulders and said, "What can they do me?" And Morris had a point.

What could they do you? Here a teen-ager was called a youthful offender and got slapped on the wrists. Siberia was far away and long gone.

"Morris is funny," Ernst said. "But there's worse than him around. Look at Joseff. That kid is really bad news."

Alec heard the mention of Joseff's name and winced, as if he had heard a sour sound on the stereo. He controlled the urge to slam the ball across the room, as he controlled so many of his urges. But he slammed the paddle down just a little bit too hard, just a little bit too loudly. The gym. That would be the best place to work out his feelings. He kept his voice calm.

"See you guys later," he said. "I'm going to shoot a few baskets."

Alec had the gym to himself. He bounced the ball furiously as though he were angry with it. Funny, he thought, he wasn't mad at anybody. Not really. Except maybe fate or whatever it was that made things happen to people. Sometimes you just felt like hitting out or screaming. But you couldn't do that. So you ran hard and fast or you drove your car out on the parkway or you slapped a ball around.

"All alone, kid?" a teasing voice called. "Want somebody to play with?"

Alec dropped the ball and ran to Felicia. He hugged her long and hard and buried his face in her thick dark hair.

"You play nice," she said softly.

"Sure," he said. "I don't want you playing with any other kids on the block."

He stood there holding her and thinking of the first time he saw her. He had been in this country only a week or so. He had wandered into Beachside Y because he had heard that it was a place to make friends. He didn't notice her at first. The place was a blur of new faces and strange voices.

He had shaken hands and said "I'm Alec," and then after a while he had slapped palms and said "Call me Al." Hands, faces, and names floated around disjointedly in his mind. It would take awhile before all these strangers came together and became real people.

His throat had grown very dry and he had left the lounge to get something to drink. A soft drink machine stood in the hall, advertising with pictures the treasures hidden inside. Alec didn't know all the American soft drinks yet, and he wasn't familiar with American coins. He fumbled with the coins and the slot. Then she touched his arm and said softly, "Come, Alec. Let me show you how."

Only then did Alec really see the exciting girl with the long, dark hair. If she hadn't made the first move, hadn't led him to her gently, he might never have noticed her. And in some ways she had gently, so very gently, taken the lead ever since. There was that same gentle lead-taking in the way his mother treated his father.

Alec kissed Felicia's hair and touched his lips to her ear.

"Hey, you know something?" he whispered. "You're the best thing that's happened to me in this country."

"Better than color TV?"

He laughed. "The hell with that. And the hell with American cars too. You're the best-made item in America I ever found."

"Well, maybe like the song says you better shop around."

"Uh, uh," he said. "I don't have to. Besides, I'm too busy."

He ran his lips along her cheek and pressed his mouth to hers. They held the kiss a long time, the gym and the world around them fading far away.

Suddenly there were footsteps in their world, bringing them back to the hard, noisy gym floor.

"Hey," Mike's voice yelled loudly. "This is a raid."

Felicia and Alec broke apart and laughed.

"Okay," Alec said. "We'll go quietly."

They waved and walked down the hall hand in hand. They followed the sound of the music and walked into the lounge. Some kids were sitting and listening and some were dancing. Felicia and Alec headed straight for the dance floor.

They moved to the music of Native Son. Felicia sang the lyrics quietly to herself as she danced.

> *We walk on the wet sand*
> *Sea birds and me.*
> *Cold rain on the water.*
> *Cold rain on the sea.*

Alec loved to dance. But even more he loved to watch Felicia as she danced. He loved to watch her move, to watch her toss that long, thick, dark hair, to watch her face and body express every beat.

The record ended and someone put on a slow ballad. Alec took Felicia in his arms. They moved smoothly together. Alec put his arms around Felicia's waist. She locked her arms around his neck and they danced silently. Then Alec felt a hand tapping his shoulder.

"May I cut in?" Joseff asked sarcastically.

Alec turned to the tall, muscular, blond boy, then turned back wordlessly. Felicia and Alec kept dancing. "No," Felicia answered dreamily. "I'm not here. Go find somebody with both feet on the ground."

"What's wrong?" Joseff sneered. "Your boy friend afraid if I cut in, I'll cut him out?"

"No way, man," Alec retorted. "No way I'm afraid of that. But you heard the lady. The lady said no."

Alec tried to keep his voice light. Don't get uptight, he told himself. You're supposed to stay loose, play it mellow and easy. But he clenched his hands together, and Felicia could feel the pressure against her back. She moved away gracefully and slid one arm around Alec's waist. He followed her lead and put his arm around her.

"I'm so popular tonight," she kidded in a southern accent. "I feel just like Scarlett O'Hara." She waved her hand across her face as though it were a fan. "My, but it's warm in here. I think I need some air. Al, would you join me please?"

"Of course, Scarlett," he said.

Alec and Felicia walked out of the lounge arm in arm. Alec knew what Felicia had done. She had felt him growing tense on the dance floor. She had tried to ease the tension, and she had pulled it off.

They walked to the outer lobby. The music from the lounge grew dimmer and faded out.

"Let's dance, Al," Felicia said.

"We have no music."

"Who needs music?"

She began dancing, tossing her head and whirling her peasant skirt. The girls were wearing that style this summer. Wide peasant skirts and blouses with elastic that bared their shoulders. It had a gypsy look to it. But Felicia had a gypsy quality to her anyway. The way she moved, danced, and laughed. The happiness, the gaiety. She was so like his mother. They even looked alike. Funny, a guy picking a girl like his mother. Like father, like son.

Alec put his arm around Felicia. "Let's go out awhile," he said.

He led her outside. They sat down on the stone steps of the Y, in the corner, and leaned against the ledge.

"Did Joseff bug you in there?" she asked quietly.

"A little. I don't like the guy. Never did. I didn't like his high-handed attitude when I first came here. And I don't like hearing that you used to go with him. How'd you pick a creep like that anyway?"

It was bad enough that Felicia had gone with a boy before him. It had to be a conceited, nasty troublemaker.

Felicia held Alec's hand tight. "Joseff wasn't like that when I met him. He had just come here, and believe it or not he was quiet and shy. But then he freaked out. Got into trouble and got to be nothing but trouble. It was over long before I knew you."

"He doesn't act like it's over."

"He's just being a pain, Al. But it's over, and gone is gone."

Alec knew it was silly. Being jealous of a girl's past. But in Russia you didn't go from one boy-girl relationship to another. You didn't date and play the field the way they did here. He couldn't get used to the casual dating. It was too disposable, like those American soda cans.

"Come on, baby," she said. "Are you jealous?"

"A little."

"Well, good," she teased. "Then you won't let me get away." She moved behind him and locked her arms around his neck. "I won't let you get away either. Just you try."

"Who's trying?" he asked.

She slid around him and sat on his lap, her arms still around his neck.

"Well, then," she laughed. "I won't have to fight you." The way she flirted, teased, kidded around, the way her dark eyes spoke. It was so like his mother. If Mama were younger today, if she were seventeen and American, she would look this way. She would wear her hair long and straight and free, and she would be free, with no cares and nothing tying her.

"You know, Felicia," he confided, "you remind me a lot of my mother."

"Funny," she said. "You don't act like you're with your mother."

"You know what I mean."

She nodded. "Sure I do. And thank you, Al. Your mother's very pretty."

"Yeah, and she used to be cheerful all the time. But now it's getting rough at home. Papa is out of work and Mama got a job. She's doing social work for JARA, the Jewish-American Russian Alliance."

"That's a good job. And what's wrong with a woman working?"

"Nothing. Lots of women work in this country. In Russia too. But it seems that when families come here from Russia it's harder for the man to find work."

"I know."

"And I tell you, Felicia, one thing's for sure. There's one thing that's the same anywhere in the world. It's hard for a man if a woman supports him."

"I guess so. My Mom was always complaining that Dad didn't support us well enough. He kept studying for this degree and that and working in book stores. They fought since the day I was born and they're still at it. That's why I try to stay out of the house."

He kissed her. "I know it's rough. It's hard to make a living. But I have to find a job soon. I need extra money for college. It's important that I make good."

"You will."

Alec stayed quiet. Here he was talking about getting a

job and helping put himself through school. Alec and everyone else had tried hard to find summer jobs before school closed. Then they had looked around during the summer. But there were so many kids and so few jobs. Still, he hadn't really knocked himself out job hunting. The summer had come and gone and here he was hanging around the Y. Here he was dancing and fooling around with his girl. His father would have tried harder. His Grandpa would never have let himself have any fun at all. Alec was like the men in his family, but there was a streak of his mother in him. Being with Felicia made him feel lighthearted and good and he liked the feeling.

Felicia jumped in Alec's arms. He could feel her shudder before he heard the scuffling sounds. He turned around. About five Spanish kids were moving around on the beach block a little past the doorway. Joseff walked out. He went past Felicia and Alec without seeing them. One of the Spanish kids stepped forward to talk to Joseff. It was dark and Alec couldn't see much. From where he and Felicia sat they could only hear snatches of the conversation between the two boys.

"It's our community," the Spanish kid said.

"Forget it," Joseff ordered. "We're taking over."

"Cutting in," the Spanish kid said. Alec couldn't make out the rest.

"Yeah," Joseff was saying. "What about one of our boys being cut today?"

"Not over," Alec heard the Spanish kid say.

Alec looked at Felicia. He wanted to get her away from here in case any trouble broke out.

"Let's take a walk on the boardwalk," he said. "We've been sitting long enough."

"Okay, Al."

They got up and walked toward the boardwalk. The Spanish kids walked slowly toward them, as if to block the path. Alec looked at them. Now he could see more clearly. Now he could glimpse the tall, wiry, dark-haired kid. Now, beneath the streetlight, he could see who Joseff was talking to, who the leader was. He waved.

"Hi, Joe," he said calmly. "What's happening?"

"Hi, Al," he answered. "Nothing's happening for you to worry about."

"Who's that, José?" one of the Spanish kids asked.

"My friend. Let the guy alone. He's okay."

Felicia and Alec walked onto the boardwalk.

"How do you know him?" Felicia asked.

"We were both new at Hayes High the same week. He had transferred from some other school. The teacher gave us a cardboard tag so the kids would know our names. I didn't know Spanish and I went over and read his name. I said 'Hello, José,' like the J was for Jim or John. I didn't know it sounded like H in Spanish."

"What did he say?"

"He laughed and corrected me. I tried but I couldn't get it right. Then I said, 'I am Alec, but call me Al.' He smiled and said, 'Okay, then just call me Joe. It's easier.' We get along fine ever since."

"Well, that's good. Then we ought to be out of the line of fire."

Alec laughed. He didn't really think Felicia was serious. He didn't really feel any danger from the Spanish kids. Not for himself anyway. He had no beef with them. He figured they shared a lot of the same troubles he had. Besides, he was safe in Brighton. Joe was his friend and Joe was the top man.

Felicia and Alec stood on the boardwalk. The moon

shone on the ocean and the tide was high. The autumn sea breeze whipped the waves and chilled the air. It felt good against Alec's face. He drew Felicia to him to shelter her from the wind.

The sounds of the sea and wind blotted out approaching footsteps.

"Hi, guys," Morris greeted them. "How are you doing?"

Alec turned. "Fine," he answered. "Just fine."

"I got some stuff here that can make you feel real fine." He took out a handful of pill vials. "Good candy. Any color you want."

"No, thanks," Felicia said. "We're feeling fine enough."

"We sure are," Alec agreed. "Anyway, how come you're selling out in the open like this? You'll get busted for sure."

Morris shrugged. "What can they do me?" He waved and walked on.

Alec shook his head. "That Morris is too much. And those pills. Ups. Downs. Arounds. I don't need that stuff." He kissed her hair. "I've got my girl."

She smiled. "Right. And I'm enough trouble for you. Anyway, Al, you'll never get into real trouble. Not like Joseff or Morris. Never."

He looked out at the ocean. Felicia was right. He never would get into trouble. He would never let himself. He had been brought up with too tight a rein. In his family you didn't do anything to ruin your future. You got Americanized. You smoked a little grass. You fell for a girl. He held his face to the wildly moving air. But when you were raised as he'd been you didn't throw caution to the ocean winds.

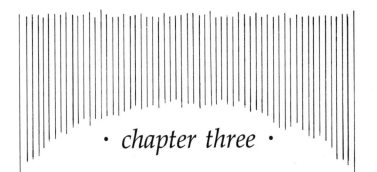

· chapter three ·

Alec finished his morning exercises. He did them faithfully, starting each new day just as he had back in Russia. He leaned out the window and inhaled deeply. It was a beautiful day. Unusually warm for this time of year. Alec stood in front of the window for a few minutes. Then he left his room and walked into the kitchen. Natasha sat alone at the table drinking milk and eating a cream-filled cake.

"Hi, little one," he said. "What are you doing here all alone?"

"I guess everybody had breakfast early. I don't know where they went."

Alec shook the percolator. Someone had already made

coffee. He turned on the flame under the pot, poured some cold cereal and milk into a bowl, and pulled his chair near Natasha.

"Look at what you're eating," he said. "What kind of breakfast is that?"

"It tastes good," she replied.

"Maybe. But it's not good for you. How will I ever get you off that American junk food?"

Natasha wrinkled her nose and rolled her tongue around the cream filling.

"Everybody eats these in school," she said.

Alec got up, poured his coffee, and sliced a banana into his cereal. He sat down and shook his head. Kids and their diets. It was a wonder they could survive in America. Natasha had a sweet tooth that wouldn't quit. Ten years old and hooked on color TV and junk food. Well, maybe the habit would be easier to cure than Morris's pills.

The phone rang and Alec walked into the foyer to answer it.

"Good morning," Felicia said. "Isn't it a great morning?"

"It sure is," he said. "And last night was great too."

She laughed. "I meant the weather. It's so warm today."

"Yeah. How come? In Russia it never gets warm in September. In the fall it just keeps getting colder and colder."

"Well, there are some warm days in autumn here. It's called Indian summer."

"That was nice of the Indians," Alec observed.

"I never thought of that. Anyway, how about playing in the sand with me today?"

"Sure. I'll get my pail and shovel and come right over."

Felicia laughed. "Make it an hour, Al. I have to straighten up, and I'm baby-sitting for Paul. Mom got a call from a temporary agency. She's filling in for a bookkeeper this morning."

"Okay, Felicia. See you in an hour."

"We can meet at the beach."

"Great. See you then."

Alec hung up and was walking back toward the kitchen when the doorbell rang. He opened the door. A cute little kid with dark straight hair and big eyes stood in the hallway.

"Come on in, Senina," he invited her. "Natasha is in the kitchen. We're finishing breakfast."

He pulled up another chair for Senina and poured her a glass of milk.

"Here, Senina. Join us. It's good for you."

Natasha handed Senina another cream-filled cake. Senina broke off half and left the rest for Natasha.

"We'll share it," she said.

"You, too," Alec said. "I just got through telling Natasha that stuff isn't good for you."

Kids. It didn't matter where they came from. Russia, Puerto Rico. It was the same. One foot in America and they're eating all the junk food in sight.

"Alec's always telling me that," Natasha said.

"Your brother's nice," Senina said.

Natasha smiled and nodded. Her blue eyes always smiled with her.

"You know what?" Senina said.

"What?" Natasha asked.

"My brother Juan is practicing football with his friends. He says that's what you do in America in the fall. Is that true?"

"I think so," Alec said.

"Well, I asked him to teach me," Senina said. "And you

know what? He said football is a boy's game. Girls couldn't play it. That's not fair. Girls are just as good as boys. I thought everybody knew that in America."

"Sure," Natasha said. "In Russia too. Girls and boys play a lot of the same sports. Girls are as good as boys. Isn't that true, Alec?"

"Sure it's true," Alec agreed.

"Then you'll teach us to play football?" Senina said. "We can go down right now."

Alec laughed. "Hey, hold on. I can't right now. I have to meet my friend at the beach soon."

"Okay," Senina said. She turned to Natasha. "I guess we'll have to play plain old ball today."

"Come on." Natasha got up from the table. "I'll get a jump rope too. The other kids must be outside by now."

Natasha and Senina waved and ran out. Alec poured himself a second cup of coffee. He remembered the first time Natasha had brought Senina around. They had been here only a few weeks. Natasha fitted in immediately. She was popular and she played with all the little kids on the block. One day she came home from school with Senina. "This is my friend Senina," she had said simply. After Senina had gone home one of the kids in the building rang the bell. The whole family had been sitting together in the living room.

"Hello, Rebecca," Natasha had said. "Come on in. 'Happy Days' will be on TV soon."

Rebecca had stood in the middle of the living room with her hands on her hips like a scaled-down version of an angry schoolteacher.

"I didn't come to watch TV," Rebecca had said. "I just want to know why you brought her around."

"Who?"

"Senina. That's who. Or whatever her name is."

"She's my friend," Natasha had answered.

"But she's Puerto Rican. How come she's your friend?"

"She's nice to me. If a kid is nice, then we're friends. If not, then we're not friends."

Alec had looked at his parents. They had been sitting silently, exchanging glances, waiting, wondering how and when they would handle this. But they didn't have to handle a thing. Natasha had handled it perfectly. That kid was beautiful.

Alec got up and washed his dishes. Out of the mouths of babes, he thought. Too bad nobody was listening.

Alec went out jogging along the boardwalk for a while. Then he came back to get ready for the beach.

"Hi," he called as he shut the door behind him. "Anybody home?"

Nobody answered. Alec started walking past the foyer wall that led to the kitchen archway. He stopped and backed up. His parents were standing near the sink doing the dishes. They must have come home and eaten lunch while he was jogging. Mama sometimes stopped at the house during the day. The running water had drowned out the noise of Alec's entrance. The water intermingled with the sounds of the small radio atop the cabinet. Mama liked to listen to music while she worked in the kitchen. A soft, romantic ballad with a background disco beat was playing. His mother danced, whirling around in a slow, gracefully seductive rhythm. She put out her hand, reaching for her husband.

"Come on, Isaac," she smiled. "You were always such a good dancer." The wet soapsuds clung to her hands and her rings.

Her husband did not take her hand. "In the kitchen?" he asked. "Don't be silly."

She tossed her head, laughed, and kept on dancing solo.

"The kitchen. The bedroom. What difference? You do what you feel."

Alec stood still, not moving from the spot. He didn't want to interrupt his parents, to make them aware that they were not alone. There was something important going on in that kitchen. Alec could sense it.

"Well, I don't feel like dancing," Papa said, "not in the kitchen anyway." He turned back toward the sink, which stood against the side wall of the kitchen.

Mama smiled and picked up a handful of soapsuds. She shaped her mouth as though she were blowing a kiss. She blew the suds toward Papa like a little kid playing with a bubble wand in early spring.

"The kitchen's not the only room in the house, you know. There can be music in our room too." She danced slowly, moving nearer to her husband, almost touching him. He turned fully toward the sink, his back to her, and turned his full attention to washing the dishes.

Mama stopped dancing. She stood still and silent in the middle of the kitchen floor. Her face, so alive and young a moment ago, looked worn, defeated, and terribly hurt. She walked slowly toward the sink and picked up the bottle of dishwashing liquid. She tried to keep her voice light and airy, to continue doing the dishes just as she had been doing earlier, just as though nothing had happened.

"I saw the funniest TV commercial about this," she said.

"Oh, what was that?"

"Well, the woman was washing the dishes and suddenly, pouff, a handsome man popped up from out of nowhere. He handed her a bottle of Bright and told her he had come to help brighten her life. That magic in American TV commercials is something to see."

"Well, maybe that's what you need, Sonia," Papa said. His voice was flat.

"What? A new bottle of Bright?"

"No," he said. His voice was still flat but it held a cutting edge of sarcasm. "No. Maybe you need a new man to help brighten your life and make magic."

Mama bit her lip and said nothing. She put the bottle of Bright on the sink and picked up the dish towel. Only the mechanical voice of the DJ broke the stark silence. Mama dried as Papa washed. Both their backs faced the side wall of the kitchen. Alec tiptoed past, quickly and quietly, and went to his room. He sat on the edge of his bed, his chin in his hands.

In Russia Papa would never have spoken to Mama that way. Not ever. Not in that tone of voice, and in those sharp, hurting words. "Maybe you need a new man." It was almost impossible to believe that those words had passed Papa's lips.

How could this be happening? True, there was always a personality difference between Mama and Papa. But Mama's fun-loving ways and Papa's seriousness never caused problems before. They seemed to blend and things were somehow okay. But now Papa was more than serious. Now Papa was becoming downright grim.

Maybe today's blowup had something to do with the kitchen atmosphere, Alec thought. Maybe it was doing the dishes that set Papa off. In Russia, and even here, his folks had always shared household chores. Everybody did. It was no big deal. But Papa was working then. Now he had no job. Now his wife worked, and the only steady work he could count on was in the kitchen.

Alec wished he hadn't walked in when he did. He wished he had missed that whole scene. It was too intimate for anyone else to have witnessed.

But he'd have to be blind and deaf not to be able to tell what was happening. Not to know that the job problems his father was having were affecting his parents' marriage every which way. Not to know what a high price they were paying for moving to this country. A guy would have to be pretty dumb not to understand this about his folks. And he'd have to be icy cold not to hurt for them deep down inside.

The low feeling stayed with Alec all the way to the beach. He headed for the spot as though he were on automatic pilot. The crowd gathered on the same stretch of sand. Meeting a friend at the beach meant walking along the boardwalk to the second entrance, going down the ramp, and following an invisible straight line two-thirds of the way toward the water.

Felicia sat alone on a blanket, looking out at the ocean. Alec ran to her, kneeled on the blanket quietly, and kissed the back of her neck.

"Robert Redford," she said firmly. "You're late."

Alec sat beside her and put his arm around her.

"So. You made a date with Robert Redford. I can't leave you alone for a minute."

She leaned her head on his shoulder. "Then don't," she said.

Alec looked at his girl. She wore a two-piece swimsuit, softly printed in shades of blue and rose, the sides of the shorts tied in narrow bows at each hip. She looked so pretty. It felt good to be near her, to see and touch her, to feel and smell the freshly shampooed hair brushing against his shoulder. The day seemed new and alive once more. They sat watching the ocean, quiet and still and all, all alone—for about two minutes.

"Hey," Mike called loudly. "You guys think you own the beach?"

Debby's transistor blared.

You kept me safe and warm
When the winter winds blew.

And those sweet kisses
That were gonna last a lifetime through
Vanished with the summer sun
Like a snowman in July.

"Looks like we've got company," Alec said. He waved. "Hi, Mike. How are you, Debby?"

"Okay," Debby said. "Hi, Felicia."

Felicia smiled and waved. Mike and Debby spread out a towel about two inches from Felicia's blanket. They didn't sit on it though. Debby just rested her transistor on the towel.

"Hey," Alec said. "That radio's so loud you can't hear yourself talk."

Mike cupped his hand behind his ear jokingly. "What's that?" he yelled.

Mike and Debby danced on the sand. Debby's strawberry blond hair shone in the sun. Rorie Brown was finishing her number, "Snowman in July." The DJ's voice was shrieking, but Mike and Debby went on dancing as though the music had never stopped. They didn't seem to notice when another record began.

Sunlight danced on blue water
Like sparkling coins of gold.
Then faded with the sunset
Like all the lies she told.
Cold rain on the water
Swelling the tide.
Chilling the morning.
Cold sadness inside.

Ernst and Becky came down, waved, and joined Mike

and Debby on their dance floor in the sand. Then Morris came running down the beach, a bunch of kids trailing behind him. They pulled up in front of Alec and Felicia. Suddenly a huge beach ball was flying around the air. It flew Felicia's way. She reached up, caught it, and threw it back.

"Don't you see the sign?" she laughed. "No ball playing on the beach."

Morris shrugged. "More rules," he said. "What can they do me?"

Alec stood up and held out his hand to Felicia. "Looks like we're in the middle of a beach party," he said. "Let's get out of here before they start roasting marshmallows."

Felicia smiled. "I don't think the sand is hot enough," she said.

They left the blanket and walked down to the ocean, following the water's edge.

"What's the matter, Al?" Felicia asked. "Not in a party mood today?"

"No," Alec said. "Not with a whole lot of people at my party anyway."

The beach wasn't as crowded as it was in summertime, but there were people all around. Some alone, some with families and friends. The neighborhood people came down any time of year, weather permitting. But the shore front was quiet enough. It was too cool for most people to be swimming. You could stroll along the shore line for a long, long stretch.

"You seem down today, Al," Felicia said. "Anything special?"

"There was a bad scene between my folks this morning," Al said. "It's rough. I hoped things would get better. But instead they just seem to be getting worse."

"Well, your family came to another country. You've got a right to figure things will get better. Me, I grew up in Brighton with my folks yelling at each other all the time. I'm still in Brighton. My folks are still yelling. But at least I never figured anything would change."

"Well, things can always change, Felicia," Alec said.

Felicia shrugged. She looked down at the sand. Her face told Alec that she didn't feel like talking about her home life. Not right this minute anyway. He held her hand tightly as they walked in silence. Felicia rolled her toes around the calmly breaking waves.

"See that white foam, Al? Just as the waves break and roll out again. You know what that foam really is?"

"What, Felicia?"

"The mermaids are swimming under the water. Too far away and deep for us to see them. They splash around when they swim and their sea foam rolls out to shore with the breaking waves."

"Where'd you hear that?" Alec asked.

Felicia looked out toward the ocean. "My father told it to me when I was little," she said dreamily. "He told it just that way. He said it was an old folk tale, and that there was nothing wrong with believing old folk tales."

"It is a pretty story," Alec said.

"Dad always told pretty stories," Felicia said. "He still does. He reads and he remembers and he tells pretty stories."

Alec nodded and moved nearer to Felicia. They walked together quietly as the water rolled slowly. They paid no attention to the distance they had walked. Then a jarring rhythm shattered the quiet time. Alec and Felicia looked back toward the beach. A bunch of kids were sitting together, a radio and drums beside them on the sand.

Someone in the crowd lifted a hand, waving and motioning. Alec looked more closely. He walked nearer.

"Hi, Joe," he smiled. "How are you doing?"

"Okay, Al," he replied. "Welcome to our place." He laughed. "Bet you never knew where the PR's hang out."

Alec smiled. "No. I don't remember seeing you on the beach this summer. It's funny. We come to the beach all the time."

It really wasn't funny, Alec thought. Not when you stopped to think about it. It was like staked-out turfs. Little islands in the middle of a larger island. The Russians in one spot, the Puerto Ricans in another, separated by distance and an invisible "no trespassing" sign.

Alec looked around. A group of kids on bongos accompanied the Latin beat of the radio music. They were really good. The kids had an original sound. Couples danced on the sand, moving to the steady rhythm.

The music stopped for a moment. The kids stared motionless at Felicia and Alec. The welcome sign sure wasn't strung across the sand. But José was welcoming the couple and José's word stood. The music started up again.

Felicia watched one couple dancing. "I never saw that step," she said.

"It's a salsa beat," José said. "Hot sauce in English. Come on, try it with me. It's not hard."

Felicia followed José carefully, moving gracefully along with him, not missing a step of the unfamiliar dance. She and José danced until the record ended.

"Great," José smiled. "You're pretty good for an American."

"I learn fast," Felicia said.

"You sure do. I'll teach you some more steps."

"Joe," Alec laughed, "I don't want any guys teaching Felicia too much. She's my girl."

José smiled. "Okay, Al, okay. I got the picture. Don't sweat it, I never mess with a friend's girl."

"Thanks for the dance lesson, Joe," Felicia said. "I like the beat."

"We play Latin music most of the time," José said. "We never do seem to get used to American rock."

Felicia took Al's hand. "I'll teach you some of Joe's steps, Al," she promised.

"Sure," Alec said. "Next time we're dancing. It looked great."

José looked at Al and Felicia. "You two have something real good going," he said. "Anybody can see that."

"We do, Joe," Alec said. "We sure do."

"You're very lucky."

"When I'm with Felicia I feel lucky." Al looked at José. "But the way things are you have to try hard. And sometimes if you try real hard you can make your own luck."

José met Alec's eyes and nodded. "I know what you mean, man," he said.

Felicia smiled. "We should be heading back now. Before we walk to the Pacific ocean."

"That would be a long walk," Alec said.

"Thanks again for the lesson, Joe," Felicia said. She began heading toward the shore.

"Anytime." José waved to Alec. "Later, man," he called softly.

When Felicia and Alec got back to their spot the weather had begun changing, Debby's transistor was off, and the crowd was packing up to leave.

"What's this?" Alec inquired. "Everybody's leaving just because we came back."

Mike folded his arms in front of him and pretended to shiver. "It's cold, man, cold," he said.

"Roy," Alec said, "in America everybody's always cold. It's hard to figure why they buy those expensive freezers all the time."

Mike waved. "Well, if you're so hot-blooded, you stay. Maybe you can join the Polar Bear Year-Round Swim Club."

Alec turned to Felicia. "Are you cold?" he asked. "Do you want to leave?"

She shook her head. "No. You can keep me warm." She sat on the blanket, still holding his hand.

"I'll do my very best," he said, sitting down beside her.

They waved as their friends left the beach, then turned to face the water. Alec put his arm tightly around Felicia. People still sat in scattered groups along the beach.

"I just didn't feel like going home yet," Felicia said quietly.

"I know what you mean."

"No. You haven't always felt that your home was a place to keep away from."

Felicia was right. In Russia home was a warm place to come back to even in the coldest of times. And in America the family feeling warmed the cold strangeness of a new place. At first anyway. But warmth wasn't something you packed in a suitcase and took with you. It wasn't something that stayed where you placed it like a piece of china that remained in the family throughout the years. Alec was growing frightened for his family.

"Was it always that way for you, Felicia?" he asked. "Was it always so bad at home?"

"Most of the time. I love my parents. They're great when there's only one of them around. But together they're impossible."

"What do you mean?"

"It was always great being with Dad. He would wander around book stores all day when he wasn't working in them. He would read to me and tell me stories all the time. It was always a dreamy and beautiful world being with Dad. And Mom was great too. She loved to go shopping. She loved to buy pretty things. But there was never enough money. She kept yelling that Dad wasn't trying to make a decent living. They hardly ever quit fighting to this day."

"Things will get better," Alec said.

"When? I'll start college in a year. I don't know what I'll major in yet but at least I'm on my way out. I worry about Paul though. He's only seven, and he covers his ears all the time to keep out the noise of the fighting."

"That's really rough, Felicia," Al said. "But things will get better. We'll make them better. You'll see. The way it is with our parents now. It won't be that way with us."

Felicia pressed her cheek against Alec's. He looked out at the ocean and thought of that night in Russia. The night the family decided to cross this very ocean in hopes of a better life. "Each generation makes the next one better," his father had said. They work, they try to do their best for their children, they suffer and hurt and wear scars. For the future. For the next generation.

He looked down at Felicia. They were growing up. Soon there would be another generation. And maybe they could do it. Maybe there was hope. His parents had left their home for their children. Maybe the generation to follow would have a better life. Maybe he and Felicia could make it together.

Felicia moved against Alec's shoulder. "Look, Al," she said. "Look over there. A sandstorm is heading this way."

Alec looked toward the far end of the beach. The

sandstorm, very common on the beach in the fall, was moving quickly in a straight path toward them.

Everyone picked up their belongings and rushed from the beach, like a camp of gypsies on the run.

"Let's wait it out, Al," Felicia said.

"Sure. Why not?"

They watched the sand fly up and move horizontally along the beach like snow in a wind-whipped blizzard. When the storm neared them Felicia and Alec covered their bodies and faces with the blanket and lay buried in the sand. In moments the wind stopped, the blowing sand passed them and moved on, and the beach was quiet, calm, and empty.

Felicia poked her head out of the blanket. "Look, Al, we're all alone on the beach."

"You're right," he said. "Just what I always wanted. A desert island all to myself."

"All alone?" she asked.

"No, baby," he said. "Not all alone."

He kissed her tenderly, then longer and harder. She held on to him tightly. Always before Alec had held back. Always before Alec had kept a rein on his lovemaking. It was a carry-over from his days in Russia. You had to be married first, or at least very nearly married. But Felicia was his girl now. His strongest link to the future. Now, alone on the long, long stretch of golden sand, now, alone with the sounds of the rolling waves and the singing gulls, Alec felt closer to Felicia than ever before.

He moved his hand gently along her side and touched the bow of her swimsuit. He fumbled for the knot, suddenly feeling awkward as his fingers shook on the soft fabric. Felicia undid the narrow string and pressed Alec's hand tightly. Then she drew him to her.

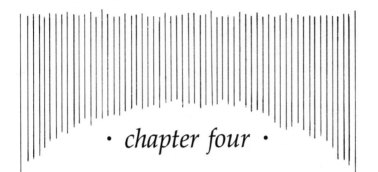

· *chapter four* ·

The September sun shone brightly for days. Everything seemed shinier to Alec. The new closeness he felt for Felicia made the whole world a friendlier, more cheerful place to be. Things seemed better between his parents too. Alec never knew what went down but after that morning in the kitchen the strain seemed to lessen a little. It was as though the downhill slide of their marriage had hit them, and they were trying hard to stop it from happening.

Alec looked out at Sunday morning. It was warm and the sun glowed as though it had never set the night before. Alec headed for the phone to call Felicia.

"Wake up," he said. "It's a great day and you should be with me, right now."

"I'd love to, Al," she said. "I really would. But Mom is going to see some women she used to work with. Dad seems a little low. He's taking Paul out for the day and they want me to go along."

"Sure, you go ahead. Paul will feel better. I'll just hang around with my folks today."

"How about calling me tonight, Al?" she asked. "We'll be back by then."

"Okay," he said. "I guess I can wait if I really try."

She laughed. "See you later."

Alec went downstairs. The little kids were already up and out and well into the day. Natasha and a group of kids were jumping rope on the sidewalk. Senina was standing in the shade waiting her turn to jump. She walked up to Alec.

"Did you want to teach us football today, Al?" she asked.

"Well, I hadn't figured on it, but I guess I could give it a try."

"I hope you don't mind, Al," she said in a serious voice. "But I just don't feel like football today. Everybody's playing rope. Maybe next time if that's okay."

He smiled. "Sure, Senina. Whatever you say."

Senina went back to her spot. Natasha jumped in. She looked graceful and so full of life. Her dark, curly hair bounced with the rhythm of the jump rope rhyme. She kept the rhythm and never missed a step.

> *Ships on the river.*
> *Ships on the sea.*
> *How many miles*
> *till you sail to me?*
> *One, two, three, four.*

Alec stood watching and listening as Natasha jumped to

the singsong count. It was great to watch kids at play. A picture of Felicia flashed through Alec's mind as he watched the kids. Felicia and the future were bound together in Alec's mind. Felicia, and carefree days, and little kids at play.

"Hi, Al," Mike called.

Alec turned. "Hi, Mike. Hi, Ernst. How's it going?"

Ernst shrugged. "Up and down," he said. "I'm waiting for my marks from Hayes High. I have to pass those make-up classes or I won't graduate."

"You'll make it," Alec assured him.

"Maybe," Ernst said. "Maybe not. The waiting is rough. Everything is rough trying to make it over here. My father was a plumber in Russia. Joining the union was so tough here he had to start as a plumber's assistant. Now my parents want me to go to college, get an education, and a good job. I'm trying to make my folks proud." Ernst looked at the little kids jumping rope. "Just look at them," he said. "Not a worry in the world. It's great."

"Yeah," Alec said. "I was just thinking about that before you came by."

"It's so much easier to get used to a new country when you're their age. They pick up the new language in no time flat. They catch up with the other kids in school a lot sooner. You always knew English, Al. But I really had a time of it at Hayes."

"I know. It must be hard to worry about high school on top of all the other troubles around."

"You know," Mike said. "I never thought about it till I got to be friends with Ernst. How it would be to come to a new country at our age. It's really a rough way to go for you guys."

"Sometimes it is, Mike," Alec said.

"Yeah. Sometimes I try to picture it when I'm talking to

Ernst. How it would feel. What it would be like if my folks came to me one day and said, 'Hey, Mike, guess what? We're moving to France tomorrow,' or Italy or someplace."

Ernst smiled. "It didn't happen just like that."

"I know, Ernst," Mike said. "But sometimes I try to put myself in your place. There I am, planted in some country in Europe, knowing I'm there for good, not knowing a soul, or the language, or my way around. Not having my old friends with me. It really blows my mind."

"It's not easy," Ernst said. "I remember Joseff making fun of all the new kids who didn't join his gang."

Alec nodded. "I remember that too."

"It would have been easy to go that way, get into hassles with the Puerto Rican gangs. But I was lucky. I made good friends fast."

"You did," Alec agreed. "Mike is the best."

The doorway of the apartment house opened and the rest of the Steinoff family stood outside.

"Good day, Ernst. Mike," Papa said.

"Hello, Mr. Steinoff," Ernst said. "Nice to see you, Mrs. Steinoff."

"Hello, boys," Mama greeted them cheerfully. "Out for a Sunday stroll?"

"Just hanging around, Mrs. Steinoff," Mike said. "It's a great day."

"Yes, it is. It's so beautiful we thought we'd go for a long walk. How about joining us, Alec? Grandpa's coming too."

"Sure," Alec said, "sounds like a great idea."

Mike and Ernst walked on. "Have a good time," Ernst said.

"Thanks," Alec replied. "And you try to be cool."

"Ernst having problems?" Papa asked.

"Yes. With school. He may not graduate this year."

Mama frowned. "Always something," she observed. Then she smiled. "Well, we're walking away from troubles today. It's too pretty a day for worrying." She motioned to Natasha. "Honey," she called. "We're all going for a walk. Come on along."

Natasha left the line and waved. "My folks are all leaving," she said. "They don't want me to stay alone." She tossed her hair and looked very grown up. "I can take care of myself," she said seriously, "but I don't want them to worry."

The Steinoffs walked down the wide main street. The entire avenue was one long shopping center, not compact like a suburban mall, but lined with small stores and businesses, block after city block. The street was crowded with strollers and shoppers out on a sunny early autumn Sunday. Most stores in Brighton stayed open Sundays.

Alec glanced around him. Nobody looked like they had much money to spend. The neighborhood people were, for the most part, very far from rich. They were dressed as though they were just about holding their own, just about making it. But their clothes, their walks, their faces, seemed to say that making it was a hard way to go.

The stores and the shoppers were of different backgrounds. There were kosher-food stores, Italian pizzerias, bodegas, and oriental tea and spice shops. There were children, young families, teen-agers, and many older people, a sure sign of an area that had been around for many, many years. Alec remembered driving out to Long Island with Mike one summer day to visit Mike's sister. The place looked like a youth ghetto. Nobody was much over thirty and no houses were over ten years old.

Alec liked the tone of Brighton better. A neighborhood

should have all different kinds of people in it, all generations. Today there were many older people out, walking slowly, some holding on to each other for physical and emotional support. Some, like Grandpa, walked with their families. Grandpa walked slowly, a tall old man standing as straight as he could. But somehow, Alec could never picture him holding on to anybody. It would be too much like giving in.

The mix of people was unusual for New York and for Long Island. Alec never really got to see much of other areas, but he loved to drive, and he drove whenever anybody had someplace to go. He passed through the sights near his new home like a tourist, riding through town after town. From what Alec could see Brighton was more like the old American melting pots than any other neighborhood around. You read about the American melting pots in social studies at Hayes High. The places where European immigrants came when they landed in America years ago. Now, people were landing in America once again. The Russian Jews were moving in right along with the Puerto Ricans. Now, there was another melting pot. But Alec wondered how well the new mixture would blend.

Natasha ran about. "There's Knish Korner," she cried excitedly. "Let's go in."

Everybody followed Natasha and the delicious aroma to the large counter of the shop. Natasha didn't leave the family much choice.

"I want the potato, the blueberry, the cherry, and—"

"Hold it," Mama interrupted. "You'll eat everything in sight. Let's get one of each and share it."

The Steinoffs stood eating their knishes, along with everyone else at Knish Korner. Then they walked on. Just about three steps later Natasha ran on again.

"Oh, look," she gestured. "Creamy Custard. Can I have one?"

Alec laughed. "I don't think custard and knishes sit together too well."

Papa smiled. "Well, maybe just this once."

Natasha ran up to the counter. "Can I have the triple decker?" she asked.

"One decker will do," Mama laughed. "And that's enough nourishment for this walk."

"Okay, Mama," Natasha said.

They walked along slowly, keeping pace with Grandpa, as Natasha licked her custard, contented as could be.

Papa inhaled deeply. "You can smell the ocean from here," he said. "It seems so fresh and clean."

Alec looked up the block. You could see the boardwalk and the water from the avenue. A steady stream of people passed along the boardwalk. Everyone was out today.

"The tide is blowing the sea breeze this way," Alec said.

"Yes. It's lovely today," Papa said. "The sun, the sea breeze, the smell of the ocean. It makes you realize how important the simple pleasures in life can be. Things that nature gives us free of charge."

Alec looked at his father. It was good to see him a little more up for a change. Mama stopped at the corner, turned her face to the bright rays of the sun, then turned to the calm, clear water.

"You're right, Isaac," she said. "The sun is gorgeous and so is the water. And the blessings are free." She laughed. "You know, I remember a story my mother told about my great grandmother. It seems my great grandparents lived in a nice house near a lovely lake. Grandma used to tell Mama about the ducks that floated past the house all the time. My great grandparents weren't rich but some people thought they were. When Grandma was marrying my grandfather, the bridegroom's family asked for a dowry. Great grandma promised, and then after the wedding his family came around to collect. 'A dowry, of course,' my great grandmother said calmly. 'Just take the ducks from the water.'"

Alec laughed. "The women in Mama's family sure are something else. They were liberated way before their time."

Papa smiled. He moved to put his arm around Mama. Then his inhibitions got the better of him. Alec could read him thinking, "You don't show affection in public." Papa just moved closer to his wife and looked at her tenderly. "Nobody would ever have needed to offer me a dowry to marry you, Sonia," he said softly.

Mama smoothed her breeze-blown hair. She brought her hand down and looked at her rings for just a moment as they glistened in the sunlight.

"That's sweet, Isaac," she murmured. "But that's when I was young and pretty. How about now?"

"You're always young and pretty, Sonia," Papa said. "Always."

Mama smiled and said nothing. Alec could see the faint sadness in Mama's smile.

Then Natasha was on the run again. "Franks," she said. "Let's get a frank."

"No way," Alec said. "Didn't you hear Mama say that custard was it?"

Natasha decided to try appealing to her grandfather. "But they're kosher franks, Grandpa," she said. "Doesn't that make them okay?"

"Kosher franks are fine, Natasha," Grandpa responded. "But I'm afraid I must agree with the family. Franks will not go with knishes and custard."

"Oh, all right," Natasha said.

Grandpa looked around. "It is wonderful," he said. "The kosher butcher shops all around us here. And kosher restaurants on every block. It was so different in Russia."

"Yes," Mama said. "Do you remember how it was almost impossible to find kosher meat?"

"I can remember eating fish and more fish, going for weeks without meat, and then listening and waiting for news of a shipment. Then standing in line for hours on end just for some kosher meat or poultry. And here it's so good to see the symbols of kosher food displayed on the store fronts. Right in plain sight, instead of being hidden as in Russia."

"Yes," Papa said. "Grandpa is right."

"Let's go to the next block and walk home on the boardwalk," Mama suggested.

"All right, Sonia."

The Steinoffs walked to the corner five abreast, and turned. Papa bumped into a man who stood on the corner near a newsstand, reading part of the Sunday paper.

"Excuse me," Papa said.

"My fault," the man replied. "I shouldn't be standing and reading in the middle of the street. But I just wanted to see the Help Wanted section and the paper costs so much on Sunday."

Papa nodded. "I understand. I have an appointment with the State Employment Agency tomorrow myself."

"Well, good luck," the man said. He turned back to the newspaper.

"Come," Mama said cheerfully. "Let's go to the boardwalk."

The cheer in Mama's voice didn't show on her face. Alec looked at his father. The sun was shining as brightly as before, but the storm clouds might just as well have filled the sky. Papa had been coasting on a sunny Sunday high. And now he was coming down, crashing fast and hard.

Papa's sadness clouded the rest of the day for Alec. The night with Felicia drove away the feelings of sadness and Alec stayed out late. When he awoke next morning Mama had left for work, Natasha was in school, Grandpa was at morning services, and Papa was nowhere around. Alec kicked one slipper across the room instead of kicking himself. He had slept so soundly he had been completely out of it. He should have been awake; he should have been there for his father. He could have driven downtown with him, spoken with him, been with him. He could have waited with him at the employment office and shared his mood afterward.

Alec did his exercises, made his bed, dressed, and ate breakfast alone. He was brooding over his second cup of coffee when the key turned in the lock.

"Papa," Alec said in surprise, "you're back early. It isn't even ten o'clock yet."

His father slumped down in the kitchen chair.

"It didn't take very long," he replied tonelessly.

Alec poured a cup of coffee for his father.

"You should have woken me up, Papa. I could have gone with you."

"You didn't miss much. Dingy green walls, hard wooden chairs, and a crowd of sad, worried-looking people. I was one of the first though. I got there early. We waited in line until the place opened."

"You had to wait in line outside, Papa?"

Papa shrugged. "So? Didn't we stand in thousands of lines in Russia? What's one more line here?"

"And what happened then, Papa?"

"Well, a man interviewed me. He looked very bored. I

guess he feels that asking the same questions over and over is a boring job. But at least he has a job."

"Did he do anything for you?"

"No. He kept telling me that I wasn't entitled to unemployment insurance because I didn't work for twenty weeks. I kept telling him that I didn't want unemployment insurance. That I wanted a job, but he either wasn't listening or he didn't understand."

Alec shook his head. "That's terrible, Papa."

"Well, it's not good. But I was talking to a man while we were waiting in line. He was an accountant and his firm went out of business. He's fifty-three and he's having a hard time. They tell him he's too old. Can you imagine? Fifty-three and too old."

"What will he do?"

"He doesn't know. But he did say he heard there was a state employment agency in Manhattan that helped professional people. He's going to try them. I called and they said I could come down tomorrow."

"I'll go with you, Papa. I'll keep you company."

"Okay, Alec, if you want to." Papa rose from the chair slowly. It reminded Alec of the way Grandpa got up from his chair. In far too many ways lately Papa was reminding Alec of Grandpa. Papa was getting old, way, way too fast.

"Today is Monday," Papa said. "I guess I'll do the laundry."

In Russia the family did the laundry on Monday. But they did it together. Here Monday was becoming wash day, not work day, for Papa, and Mama was the only one with a job. It was a bad scene. But it was a worse scene alone.

"We'll go down to the basement together, Papa," Alec said.

"All right, Alec." Papa took the laundry from the

hamper and put it in a canvas bag. Alec carried the detergent and fabric softener. Then they took the elevator to the laundry room in the basement of the apartment house. Nobody else had come down yet. The laundry room was empty. Alec put everything into the washing machine, dropped two quarters into the slot, and started the wash cycle. Then he and Papa waited around until it was time to use the drier.

"Do you hear that noise?" Papa asked. "I don't mean the washer."

Alec listened. "Yes. It sounds like someone running."

Alec and Papa followed the sounds. And then they saw them. Two little kids, the oldest not more than three years old, running around the dimly lit basement, all alone.

Alec walked up to them. "Do you live here?" he asked.

The children stared blankly at him.

Papa spoke in Russian. "Where are your parents?" he asked softly.

The little boy still didn't speak. The older girl answered in Russian. "They went away," she said.

Papa kept asking questions gently, but he couldn't get any more information. The kids were alone in the basement, and they didn't know where their parents were or when they would return.

Alec put the laundry into the drier and came back. He and Papa kept talking to the kids, wondering what on earth they were going to do about them.

Mr. Golden and Mrs. Klein and her thirteen-year-old daughter Jill all came down at the same time, laundry in hand.

"Al, Mr. Steinoff," Mr. Golden said, "who are these children?"

"We don't know," Papa answered. "We've tried everything. But we can't find out. It seems they were just left here."

"I think I know," Mrs. Klein said. "A young couple moved into an apartment on our floor. They had two little ones. I think these are the children."

"Should we take them upstairs and take care of them?" Jill asked.

"Not yet," Mr. Golden said. "What if their parents come back soon? They won't know what happened to their children."

"Maybe you're right," Mrs. Klein said. "I'll wait awhile."

"I'll run up and get some toys and some cookies," Jill offered.

"That's a good idea," Mr. Golden agreed. "We'll just take turns looking after the youngsters for now."

"All right," Papa responded. "We'll help. But now I'm going down to Beachside Y to ask about a job. I'll take my turn caring for the children when I return."

"I'll go along with Papa," Alec said. "We'll be back soon."

"Sure," Mr. Golden said. "We can handle things here."

Alec and Papa walked to the Y and entered the room marked "Job Opportunities." The room was packed nearly to the door. There was no straight, orderly line. Only people, disorder, and total confusion.

"This is one big mess," Alec said.

"I would say so," Papa agreed.

Alec and Papa stood near the door. Everyone was talking at once, and they were all saying more or less the same thing: "Please, please. Get me a job."

The small agency at the Y had been set up with funds from Hebrew charities, but it was nowhere near equipped to handle this kind of crowd. Some of the pleas for jobs sounded angry and annoyed. Many of the people had never expected to have so hard a time finding work. In Russia the government gave you a job, and you did the work assigned to you. Two people applying for the same job was unheard of there, but here hundreds of people turned up for one job. The shock was terrible. A babble of voices filled the room. "Why aren't the agencies helping us?" one woman yelled. "You brought us here, where are the jobs?"

Papa wanted to go up front to speak to the interviewer, but there was no line and Papa would never push or shove. He stood politely, trying to catch someone's eye. A woman Mama knew stood up from behind a table and walked up to him.

"Mr. Steinoff, did you have an appointment?" she inquired.

"No, Mrs. Kantrowitz. I didn't realize I would need one."

"Well, I am sorry, but we try to go by appointment. As you can see it doesn't always work out."

"Yes. So many people anxious to work."

"I'm afraid so. But can you come back next week? I'll put you down for Thursday at 9 A.M."

"Surely, Mrs. Kantrowitz," Papa said. "I'll try again. Who knows? If you keep trying, one day you might succeed."

"Of course, Mr. Steinoff. Can you stop by tomorrow? I'll make out an appointment card and give it to you then. That way you can show it to any interviewer when you come next week."

"Thank you, Mrs. Kantrowitz," Papa said. "I'll see you sometime tomorrow."

Alec followed Papa as he left the Job Opportunities room

and walked slowly down the hall. They passed the Senior Citizen lounge and stopped. Grandpa often went there.

Mr. Epstein was pounding on the table. He sometimes visited Grandpa and he often pounded on tables when he talked to make his point. Mr. Epstein was a round, cheerful-looking man.

"Of course this is the land of opportunity," he was shouting. "How can you argue the point, Solomon?"

"It is a point to argue, Jacob," Mr. Leonofsky insisted. His voice and thin face were serious. "Here we have fresh fruit, but not our old friendships. Here we have freedom to walk as we choose, but no homeland."

Alec looked inside the lounge. Grandpa wasn't there yet. He was probably still in temple. Alec didn't feel like hearing discussions on the land of opportunity. Not right now. Not after the Job Opportunities room. He took his father's arm.

"Let's go home now, Papa," he suggested. "We promised to help with the little kids we found."

When Papa and Alec got back to the house nearly all the neighbors were gathered in the basement. The area around the laundry room seemed like the apartment house community meeting hall. The noisy confusion of everyone talking at once echoed through the hollow space.

"You'd think someone spread the word that this is the place to be," Alec commented.

"Yes," Papa said. "I remember one day last month. I came down to the laundry and Mrs. Karansky was sitting here on a beach chair, listening to a small portable radio. I asked her why she didn't sit outside or on the boardwalk. She said the apartment was so small. Her husband and three children were always underfoot and this was the only place to be alone."

"A basement beach," Alec observed. "That's something."

"It really is. I left Mrs. Karansky alone with her thoughts and as I did the wash I heard her saying over and over, 'They took my home. They took my home.'" Papa stared off into space and seemed to be speaking to himself rather than to Alec. "And now the whole crowd is down here. How low we must feel inside to make the basement the center of our lives."

Alec touched his father's arm. "We should see what we can do about the kids," he said.

"Yes. We must try to get some order here." Papa walked toward the crowd. "Has anyone learned where the children's parents are?" he asked.

"No," Mr. Golden said. "We have no idea."

"Then we must discuss this calmly," Papa said, "and decide what to do."

"Has anybody called the police?" Mrs. Karansky asked.

"Oh no," Mr. Golden said. "No police. Their parents may have troubles and they may have been wrong to leave the children. We don't know. But they're our people. We handle it ourselves."

Papa said nothing. Alec knew that Papa understood there was no sense in discussing calling the police. In Russia you steered clear of the authorities, and the habits and old fears were too deep to change.

Everybody else may have been upset but the kids sure weren't. They were having a ball being the center of attention at one big party. Neighbors brought down canvas chairs and small end tables. They brought hot lunch and milk for the kids and provided toys and coloring books. Everybody, including Alec and his father, read stories to the kids, played with them, and held them on their laps. Mama came home right after lunch. She had been in the neighborhood at a meeting for JARA and stopped at the house. Jill was on her way to the laundry room with toys when she met Mrs. Steinoff in the hall. Mrs. Steinoff joined the crowd after Jill told her about the kids. Everyone brought Mama up to date on the news of the morning and she pitched in and helped. A little while later a young couple walked calmly into the basement. The little kids ran to them and the neighbors watched as happy, loving hugs were exchanged.

Mrs. Klein walked up to the couple. "Aren't you the people who moved in yesterday?" she inquired.

"Yes," the man smiled. "We are the Marinskys."

"Then these are your children?" Papa asked.

"Yes," Mrs. Marinsky said. She looked around. "Where are all the other children?"

"What other children?" Mrs. Klein asked.

"The other children in your school," Mrs. Marinsky said. "You have a very nice school here. So many people helping. Are all the schools in America like this?"

The neighbors looked at each other, completely puzzled. Mama walked over to the Marinskys. "Tell me," she encouraged them patiently, "when you left the children here, did you think you were bringing them to a day-care center? To a nursery school?"

"Yes," Mrs. Marinsky said. "A school for little children. That's how it was in Russia. The school was downstairs. We went to work. We dropped the children at school on our way to work every day."

"There was a day-care center in the basement of your apartment house in Russia?" Mama asked.

"Yes," Mrs. Marinsky replied. "A school just like here."

"There are day-care centers in many large apartment

houses in Russia," Mama said. "Lots of them are in the basements. But didn't you see that nobody was here? You left your children all alone down here. That's very dangerous."

The Marinskys looked at each other. They didn't understand. "We went to look for work," Mr. Marinsky said. "We need jobs and we wanted to leave early. In Russia we sometimes left for work early."

"And when you left for work early you would sometimes leave the children alone in the basement?"

"In the school. Yes." Mrs. Marinsky smiled. "Someone would come in a few minutes to take care of the children. Someone always came."

"Yes," Mama said. "We understand. You did what you used to do in Russia. But it is not the same way here. We will explain things to you. We will help you."

Alec looked at the couple. Here they were in a brand new country with two little kids. And they were hardly more than kids themselves. They were here knowing absolutely nothing about the place. Maybe they had seen a few travelogues in a movie house. No more than that. So they thought things were the same as in Russia. You left your children in the basement. Why not? Someone would take care of them. Someone always took care of your children in Russia. You could count on it.

The innocence of the nice young couple was shocking. Until you thought awhile. Then it figured. And it figured that incidents like this would happen more and more. The Marinskys might be one of the first. But the planes from Russia would be bringing in more couples like the Marinskys. A whole lot more. And some of them might even know a whole lot less. It was going to be a problem. Another very serious problem. Mama said it first. She was speaking to the Marinskys, to the neighbors, and to herself. Thinking out loud.

"I've got to talk to the people at JARA," she said. "We're going to need classes for young parents new to America. But most of all we need day-care centers. And we need them fast."

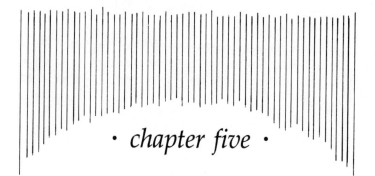

· *chapter five* ·

Everybody forgot their problems. For that afternoon anyway. The neighbors all shared in one problem. Helping the Marinskys and the kids. Finally things got straightened out. Not that anybody could get hold of a magic wand and wave away the Marinskys' troubles. It would be a long haul for the family. But the danger to the children was past.

The Marinskys understood that there was no day-care center around. The neighbors offered to take turns baby-sitting while the couple looked for work. They would all help in any way they could. Then in mid-afternoon everybody packed up their canvas chairs, toys, cookies, and went upstairs.

Grandpa had just gotten home. He had heard about the Marinskys from one of the neighbors as he waited for the elevator. "Terrible thing," he said. "A young couple having to raise babies without knowing the customs of the new country. I pray they will all be safe. I'm only sorry I wasn't here to help them."

"That's all right, Papa," Mama soothed him. "There were plenty of people to help." Mama sighed. "The little children are not our only problem," she said. "I heard disturbing talk at JARA today."

"What was that, Sonia?" Grandpa asked.

"A social worker who deals with teen-age problems came to the meeting. She said there are serious problems between Russian and Puerto Rican gangs."

"Yes," Alec said. "I'm afraid so. It's a bad scene."

"Very bad," Papa said. "Young people should be studying, not fighting. They should be trying to build a good future in their new country."

"Yes," Grandpa said. He gripped the arms of his chair. "I hear stories in my senior-citizen group too. Mr. Marcus's brother lives near Coney Island. He says old people have been robbed there and he is frightened, so he is moving to Brighton." Grandpa shook his head. "That is terrible. Young people should do what's right."

Mama stood up and pressed Grandpa's hand. "Yes, Papa. You're right. But don't get so upset. We're safe in Brighton and maybe things will get better between the youngsters." She smiled. "Let's relax, Papa. Would you like some tea now?"

"Thank you, Sonia. A glass of tea would be very nice."

Mama went into the kitchen to put up tea. She was out of the living room for quite some time. When she came back into the room her hair was loose and it had been brushed until it shone. She was wearing a long, brightly colored hostess gown that swung around her as she walked. She put the tray of tea and cookies on the living room table near Papa. She stood in front of him and stretched slowly. Her nails were covered with silvery rose polish that gleamed along with her rings. "It's been such an exhausting day," she said. "Some tea and a little something sweet should make us feel better."

Papa didn't answer. He just sipped his tea as though he didn't even notice his wife. Mama sat next to Alec and quietly poured some tea for Grandpa. Then the door opened and Natasha burst in.

"We don't have much homework," she said, throwing her books down in the foyer alcove. "Just a little math. Everybody's outside. Is it okay if I go down now and do my homework later?" Natasha didn't give anybody a chance to answer. She just went right on talking. "Chocolate chip cookies!" she exclaimed. She grabbed a handful from a dish next to Papa. She took the nearest seat, and that was Papa's lap. She just sat right down, ate the cookies in one mouthful, and hugged Papa around the neck. Then she jumped up, ran to the door, and was gone before anyone could get a word in.

Mama stood up. "I better call JARA. I have to start the ball rolling about day-care centers. The Marinsky children ought to show how badly we need day care in Brighton."

She dialed the foyer phone. "Yes. It's important. Please ask Mr. Karlin to call me as soon as he gets in."

When Mama walked back into the living room, she didn't take the seat she had left. Instead she sat down on Papa's lap, just as Natasha had done, and put her arms around his neck. "This is a comfortable chair," she said playfully. "My daughter knows where to sit. But you've got two girls in this house. Remember?"

Papa reached for the tea. He reached right past Mama. "I

guess I'll straighten up," he said. "You must be very tired."

Mama got up and crossed the room. She sat near Alec and shut her eyes for a minute. Alec wasn't sure if Mama was tired or if she was just shutting her eyes so she could shut out her world. Papa walked into the kitchen and washed the tea glasses. Alec heard the water running, then stopping. Papa left the kitchen and was passing the foyer phone just as it began to ring.

"It must be for you, Sonia," he said. "Who calls me?" He went right by the phone without picking it up.

Mama jumped up and ran to answer it. She looked as annoyed as Alec had ever seen her. She tried to keep the irritation out of her voice as she spoke on the phone.

"But, Mr. Karlin," she said, "if you had been here. Those two youngsters had no idea that they were abandoning their children." She listened awhile. "Yes. But, Mr. Karlin, we must have day-care centers here. We need them desperately. And it would do more than help parents and children. It would be creating jobs for the people who worked in the center." She listened some more. "Yes. Yes. I know. We have to go through channels. But sometimes it's like swimming upstream against the tide. All right, Mr. Karlin. I'll be there first thing in the morning and give it my best sales talk."

Mama hung up and came back to the living room. She sank down on the couch and sighed.

"What happened, Mama?" Alec asked.

"Mr. Karlin said he agreed. He said we really need day-care centers. He said that in order to get those day-care centers we need federal funds. And he also said that wouldn't be so easy."

"What will you do?"

"Well, Mr. Karlin is having me meet Mrs. Marks in Manhattan tomorrow morning. He must think two mouths are better than one. There's a federal office that hears pleas for funds."

"That's very good," Grandpa said. "Then the American government will help us."

Mama shook her head. "Mr. Karlin wasn't so sure, Papa. He warned me that lots of agencies needed federal money badly, and there just isn't enough to go around."

The old-time immigrants figured out that American streets weren't paved with gold, Alec thought. Now, the latest immigrants were finding out that the streets weren't paved with American dollars either.

"But this is such a worthy cause," Grandpa said.

"There are other worthy causes too, Papa."

"I know. And I know, Sonia, that you'll try as hard as you can."

Mama shut her eyes and opened them again. "Yes, Papa," she said tiredly. "I do try as hard as I can."

Alec awoke very early next morning. He made sure to be up and dressed before his parents were ready to leave for Manhattan. He had let his father down yesterday by being asleep instead of being with him. This time he was going to be there in case his folks needed him.

Grandpa had gone to temple and Natasha had left for school. Alec walked toward the kitchen. Mama was standing in front of the large, decorative foyer mirror. She put her hand to the neckline of her blouse and pulled it down past her neck. She kept gazing into the mirror.

"Good morning, Mama," Alec said. "How do you feel today?"

"Old," she answered simply.

"You, Mama! Old. That's the silliest thing I've heard yet."

"No. No, Alec, it isn't. Maybe last year it was silly but now things don't look the same. I don't look the same. I don't feel the same either." She turned her face upward. "Crepey neck."

"What? What do you mean, Mama?"

"Crepey neck. One of the signs of aging. Your neck gets kind of wrinkly and saggy. That's one of the TV commercials for a wrinkle cream. There's a frightening sounding voice-over where the announcer comes on and says 'crepey neck.' From the tone of his voice you might think a hurricane was coming."

Alec laughed. "Well, whatever it means, you don't have it."

"Yes, I do. I look like the before part in the before and after ad for Eternal Youth Wrinkle Cream."

"Oh, come on, Mama," Alec said. "You're a long way from needing that stuff."

"Maybe I was. In the past. But now it's starting to look like there's more past than future. For me anyway. Now it looks like the future is a time for the kids."

Alec began to feel scared. His mother never acted this way. Never spoke this way.

"Come on, Mama," Alec tried to joke. "You're just fishing for compliments. You know I've got the youngest, best-looking mother on the block."

"You learned to say the right things in America, Alec." The down tone in Mama's voice didn't change.

"You do look great this morning. That outfit is terrific. You'll knock 'em dead in that federal funding office."

"Sure. If they're half dead anyhow."

Mama wasn't kidding back, or smiling or anything. Alec would try a song and dance routine if he thought it would do any good. But Alec didn't really know what would help. Mama had been lifting everybody's spirits for so long, nobody ever thought about lifting hers. And he wasn't doing too good a job. Mama was the chief cheerer-upper in the family, and it looked like she was about to resign.

Alec turned to see Papa standing near the foyer entrance. He didn't know how long Papa had been there or how much he had seen and heard. But he must have heard something.

"You look very pretty today, Sonia," he said.

"Thank you, Isaac," Mama said. Her voice was formal, as though a passing acquaintance had paid her a compliment at a large party. She didn't turn from the mirror. Papa put his hands on her shoulders. "That yellow blouse looks lovely with your coloring," he said. "So bright and sunny."

He was trying. He knew his moods had played a part in bringing Mama down. And now he was really trying. It was hard for him and Mama knew it. Slowly she reached back, put her hand over Papa's, and pressed it tightly.

After breakfast Papa looked at his watch. "It's time to go, Sonia," he said. "Let me drive you to Manhattan."

"Why not let me drive?" Alec suggested. "You won't be able to park in midtown and I have nothing much to do today. Besides, I love to drive."

"Sure, Alec," Papa said. "If you want to."

Mama sat in the front seat between Papa and Alec. The traffic moved slowly and Brighton Beach was a long way from Manhattan.

"I hope we're not late," Papa said.

"Don't worry," Alec said. "There's plenty of time."

"The young always feel that way," Papa observed. "That there's plenty of time."

"I know, Isaac," Mama agreed. "They never feel that time is running out. And it isn't. Not for them. But sometimes I feel that time is racing and we're standing still. Getting nowhere. It's such a struggle in this country. Sometimes I wonder if it's worth it."

"Of course it's worth it, Sonia, for the future."

"Yes. You're right, Issac. For the children's future." She sighed. "I guess all we can do is hope that things will get better."

"We mustn't give up hope, Sonia," Papa said. "There is always hope."

Alec clutched the wheel tightly. His parents were living on hope. Hope for their children's future, not their own. They weren't even living for the present. So much of the joy seemed gone from their lives. They had a right to wonder if it was worth the price.

Alex exited from the parkway and drove uptown through the city streets. He was in Manhattan now and it was completely different. It was a strange thing about this country. You were in a whole different world the moment you left your neighborhood. Alec drove up past the Bowery, past the drunks pounding on the car window begging for coins, past the slum tenements of the Lower East Side, and up into the midtown business district. Manhattan seemed so cold to Alec. People rushed through crowds, going about their business in a frenzied hurry. They were surrounded by people, but there was no sense of humanity here. It seemed that everyone walked in isolation, completely encased in an invisible plastic bubble.

"We're almost at the federal funding office," Mama said.

"I know, Mama," Alec said. "I'll turn the corner and let you out."

Alec turned and pulled up at a bus stop. "I think this is the building, Alec," Mama said.

The driver's side was nearest the curb. Alec opened the door and got out of the car.

"Slide past the steering wheel, Mama," Alec said. "There's too much traffic for you and Papa to get out the other side. Besides, you're slim enough to slide over."

"All right, Alec," Mama responded.

Papa moved nearer his wife and took her hand.

"Good luck today, Sonia," he said.

Mama held Papa's eyes. "You too, Isaac," she answered softly.

Alec held out his hand for his mother.

"Such a gentleman, Alec." Mama smiled. "Don't you know we're liberated in America now?"

Alec laughed. "Yes. But I can still open a car door for my mother." He looked around. "I thought you were meeting Mrs. Marks here."

"She'll be here soon." Mama waved him away. "Go on. Go on, Alec. Your father will be late. I'll be fine."

Alec got back into the car. He kept the door open and lit a cigarette. He didn't want to drive away until he was sure his mother was safe. She had never been to Manhattan alone before and she had been there only a couple of times. Then he heard a woman's voice calling.

"There you are, Mrs. Steinoff. How is everything?" The tall, silver-haired woman came up to Mama.

"Everything could be better, Mrs. Marks. But I guess you know that. We're here to see what we can do about making things better."

"Your idea for day-care centers is a wonderful one. I hope we can convince the funding office of that."

"So do I, Mrs. Marks. But it's an uphill fight. Everything

is so uphill in this country. It's like being in labor all the time."

"Well, Mrs. Steinoff, when you're in labor you know it will end and something worthwhile will come of it."

"That's true. I wish it were true of this pain."

"You're usually more optimistic, Mrs. Steinoff. But when you talk about the day-care center plans I know your enthusiasm will come through."

"We'll do our best. Come, Mrs. Marks. It's time to go in now."

Alec watched the two women walk into the office building. He ground out his cigarette in the ash tray and shut the car door. He turned to his father. Papa was looking out at the street, looking out and away. Alec checked the rearview mirror. He pulled out and smoothly entered the flow of traffic.

Papa didn't speak until Alec stopped the car at the professional employment office. Then he sighed.

"I see that we are here, Alec."

"Yes, Papa. This is the address you gave me."

Papa opened the door slowly. "I'll see you at home later, Alec."

"I can drive around and stop back in half an hour, Papa."

"All right, Alec. If I'm through here I'll be waiting for you."

"Good luck, Papa."

Papa got out of the car. "Thank you, Alec," he said. "I will need it."

Alec drove around for a while. Then he pulled up in front of the office building where he had dropped his father and honked. Papa came out of the doorway slowly, his eyes studying the sidewalk. He got into the car as though he were carrying a heavy package.

"Papa," Alec asked, "how'd it go in there?"

"I sat and waited until a man called for me. Then I sat across from the man's desk as he asked me questions."

Alec checked behind him and drove away from the curb.

"What kind of questions, Papa?"

"Well, Alec, one of the first questions he asked me is where I live." He paused. "You know, Alec, sometimes I'm not sure."

"I know what you mean, Papa. Sometimes being here doesn't seem real."

"Yes." Papa sighed. "Then he asked what kind of work I could do. I told him I was a teacher. He looked through a lot of cards on a wheel he had on his desk. Then he copied down some information on a piece of paper and handed it to me. 'Call the office manager,' he said. 'He's got a few hours of work tomorrow morning filling in for a messenger.'"

Alec looked at his father in disbelief. "Is that guy crazy?"

"I don't think so. I told him that this was a professional office and that I was a professional person. I spoke very politely."

"Sure you did, Papa. You always do. What did he answer?"

"He just said, 'Look. Do you want the work or don't you?'"

"Oh, wow!" Alec shook his head.

"I said I wanted to work. I said I wanted to teach. I told him I could teach Russian here. He said every Russian could teach the language. And how many people here wanted to learn it?" Papa paused. "I took the job."

Alec tried to keep his voice calm. "But, Papa," he said. "You don't mean that. You're a learned man. You're a teacher and a good teacher."

"Maybe so, Alec. But nobody seems to want to learn anything I have to teach."

"Don't be silly, Papa. You! Working as a messenger even for a few hours. Tear up that paper. Papa, it's ridiculous."

Papa looked out of the window instead of into his son's eyes.

"It's a few hours of work, a few hours less that my wife will support me. I thought it might help. But so far it doesn't make me feel any more like a man."

Alec looked at his father. Papa still did not turn to face him. Alec said nothing. Maybe his father would forget it. This kind of thing was bad news. Lowering goals was never a good thing. Papa had always taught Alec that. Grandpa had always taught Papa that. Besides, they had come to this country to make their lives better. This sure wasn't making Papa's life any better.

Alec had come along to keep his parents company. But right now Alec felt that the best way to comfort his father was by quiet nearness. Alec and Papa stayed silent throughout the rest of the return trip to Brooklyn. Alec found a parking space near the house. When the car was parked Papa finally spoke.

"I told Mrs. Kantrowitz I would come to the Y this morning for my appointment card."

"I remember. Is it okay if I tag along?"

"Of course, Alec," Papa said. "Your company is always welcome."

When Alec and Papa got to the Job Opportunity room Mrs. Kantrowitz was busy. She smiled, waved Papa over to the desk, and gave him next week's appointment card.

"We'll see you next week, Mr. Steinoff," she said.

"Thank you for your trouble, Mrs. Kantrowitz," Papa answered.

When Alec and Papa passed the Senior Citizen lounge a noisy discussion was going on. Mr. Epstein was pounding on tables again. Grandpa was sitting in the lounge.

"Come in," he called. "Come join our little meeting."

The cheery looking Mr. Epstein was still arguing his case for the New World. The guy was acting like a lawyer, preparing a brief for the rose-colored glasses side.

"Many of our people are succeeding," he said. "Many have already found secure places in their new country."

"That's true," Mr. Leonofsky said. His voice grew very serious. "We do hear heart-warming stories. But we hear of heartbreak as well."

"Still, Solomon," Mr. Epstein persisted. "It is the opportunity." He pounded on the table. "The opportunity is what counts."

"Don't get so excited, Jacob," Mr. Marcus said. "It is bad for the digestion and we have just finished lunch."

"Yes, Jacob," Mr. Leonofsky said. "We trade off one set of opportunities for another. The security of an oppressive, familiar country with steady work for freedom in an unknown place."

"That is true," Mr. Marcus said. "But mostly the problems are for the younger ones, as the future is for them. For ourselves, we do not have to compete. We play cards at the Y, we talk, have lunch together here, sit on the boardwalk, and go home. So we pass our days."

"Yes," Grandpa agreed. "You are right. It is our children and grandchildren who bear the hardships. We stand by and watch our children help their children. All I can do is pray for the young." Grandpa pushed his chair back from the table, placed both hands on the table top, and got up slowly. "I will see you tomorrow," he said. "Now I think I will walk home with my family."

Three generations of Steinoffs walked along the board-walk. Grandpa walked next to his son, at his side, not touching.

"Things did not go as you hoped today, Isaac," he said. "I can tell."

"No, Papa. Nothing has changed for the better."

"Each morning and evening, when I go to shul, I pray for our family."

"I know, Papa."

Alec turned to his father and grandfather, walking beside him. Alec knew about his father's childhood, without being told. Alec knew the kind of father his father had grown up with. Grandpa was the same to his son as he was to his grandchildren. The same, always. He was sincere. He prayed for his family. He prayed. But he did not touch.

Papa tried. He really did. He tried to be different from Grandpa. To be warmer to his children. But it was hard to learn warmth. You had to grow up feeling it, and nobody had given that feeling to Papa. Papa was warmer to his children than Grandpa was, but he could not show the warmth as he would like to. The inner cold of his Russian childhood would never thaw.

Grandpa turned toward the older people, sitting together on benches, warming themselves in the sunlight and in their friendships.

"It is hard to be young," Grandpa said, "but it is not easy to be old either. People say that death makes everyone equal. But so does old age."

"How, Grandpa?"

"If you were not young, you would not have to ask, Alec. Look around. At the Y, on the boardwalk. All the old people doing the same thing. Waiting for the day to end. Maybe even waiting for the end. They use the word retire. But it is more than retiring from a job. It is retiring from life."

"Everyone seemed to be having a nice time at the Y, Grandpa," Alec said.

"But everyone becomes the same. The old have few choices. A retired doctor comes to our group sometimes. Today some people spoke of him. They did not say he is Dr. Smithline. They said of a living, breathing man, 'He was Dr. Smithline.'"

"I understand," Papa said. "They stripped him of his title, his career, and all that he had learned with one word. I met a fifty-three-year-old man who had lost his job and couldn't find another. They said he was too old. I am really beginning to understand the problems of the old."

Alec looked down at the slats in the boardwalk. Papa was doing more than understanding the problems of the old. He was beginning to feel them. He was starting to feel like a has-been in the prime of his life. Alec was afraid that if things didn't turn around soon, Papa would skip a generation, like a horrible science fiction story of whirling time.

Grandpa headed for his living room chair the moment he got home. Papa and Alec prepared a herring salad for lunch. Grandpa had already eaten. He sat alone on his chair as Papa and Alec shared their salad in the kitchen. Papa made the idle conversation of the idle.

"Is it only one o'clock?" Papa inquired, looking at his watch. "It seems so much later."

The day must have seemed terribly long to Papa. It was beginning to seem long to Alec. Long and hard. He wished it were evening and he was glad it was Tuesday. It was teen group night at Beachside and Alec couldn't wait to get there. He could talk to the kids, fool around, play Ping-Pong. He would dance, see Felicia, hold her, be with her. The dark of night would lighten the day. It would lift the heavy fog that had been rolling in since early morning.

Papa and Alec did the dishes and walked toward the living room. Grandpa was sitting in his chair, staring straight ahead. He often sat alone, looking ahead, thinking of the past.

"Do you want me to bring you a book, Grandpa?" Alec asked.

"Not right now. I was just sitting and remembering. I am an old man now. I watch pictures on the wall. Pictures of past memories. Sometimes I come back to modern times. Then I watch the electric picture box."

"I'll keep you company," Papa said.

"Of course," Grandpa said. "Will you join us, Alec?"

"Not now Grandpa. I think I'll go out for a while."

"Of course. You are young. You have so much more energy to burn."

Alec went to his room and changed to jeans and a T-shirt. He walked to the door. As he walked he passed the living room. Papa and Grandpa didn't notice him. They sat together, watching TV. As Alec walked out he could hear the station break. The announcer's voice was dramatic and serious.

"Part one of this daytime serial was brought to you by Bright soap products. Stay tuned for part two of 'Tomorrow's Hope.'"

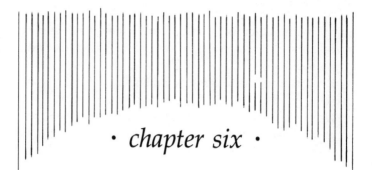

· *chapter six* ·

Alec slid his head under the pillow, covering his face against the morning light. He wanted to sleep through as much of the new day as he could. There was no stopping Papa from taking that job stint this morning. But Alec couldn't face it. He let sleep shield him from the sights and sounds of Papa's leaving.

The muffled ring on the phone cut through the pillow. Alec answered groggily.

"Sleepy head," Felicia said, "the phone rang at least eight times."

"I'm up now," Alec said. "Your voice is good to wake up to."

"I'll remember that. Now how about getting together? Mama's not working today and I have the day to myself."

"Not all to yourself," Alec answered. "How about going to the beach?"

"Okay," Felicia said. "It's cool out. But the sun is strong."

"Great. I'll meet you there."

Alec walked along the boardwalk toward the second beach entrance. People sat clustered together where the autumn sun shone most strongly. Parts of the back boardwalk, where food stand awnings shaded the sun, were nearly deserted. Alec didn't mind the chill. He walked in the silent spots, where he could hear the sounds of the sea.

Then Alec heard a clattering sound, followed by the mingling of loud and muffled voices. Alec looked around. The sounds were coming from the area of a frankfurter stand, where it was usually not crowded after the summer season. Alec walked around the side, toward the back of the stand. He recognized some of Joseff's gang, running out the back and off the boardwalk. Joseff stood, pushing an elderly man against the metal side wall of the stand.

"Who do you think you are, old man? A cop?" Joseff was saying.

"No," the man yelled, "but I'll catch those boys. I'll call the cops. Eating, and not paying the whole bill. That's terrible."

Joseff kept the man pinned hard to the wall. His back was turned to Alec, who walked up quickly and put his hand on Joseff's shoulder in a light, quick, squeezing motion.

"What's going on here?" he asked.

Joseff released his hold on the man and turned in

surprise. The man hurried back to the stand, shaking his head.

"The old guy said we didn't pay," Joseff said. "We always pay our way."

"I'll bet," Alec answered.

"You should mind your own business," Joseff said. "Or you could get into trouble."

"You're scaring me to death," Alec said sarcastically. "Pushing an old man around. That's the best you can do. The New World sure messed you up." Alec walked away.

"See you around," Joseff responded nastily.

"Not if I'm lucky," Alec called back without turning. With all the problems Alec had at home, Joseff was the least of Alec's troubles. His mind was still very much with his father.

Felicia was waiting on the beach. Nobody else in the crowd came down. It was too cool. Alec and Felicia sat alone at their usual spot wearing jeans and sweatshirts over their swimsuits. But the sand was nowhere near empty. People in Brighton came to the beach until the cold of winter set in. Some sat bundled up, sun reflectors guiding the rays to their faces. Some strolled or jogged along the beach front.

Alec put his arm around Felicia's shoulder and drew her close. He sat, holding her near, and just looked quietly straight ahead to the shore, watching the waves and the passing gulls and people.

"You're awfully quiet today," Felicia observed. "Anything wrong, Al?"

Alec didn't feel like going over it. Not just yet. He didn't feel like saying, "My father is working as a messenger right this minute and there was no way to talk him out of it." He didn't feel like saying, "I don't want to talk about it because I can't stand to think about it." So he just said, "How about some music, Felicia?"

"Sure, Al," she said. She turned on the transistor and began switching stations. The kids were always doing that. Listening to snatches of a song and then turning the dial until they found a DJ playing their favorite hit.

"Al, here's Native Son." She stopped turning the radio and nestled close to Alec. He gently tapped out the rhythm on his girl's arm as he listened to the second verse of the lyric.

> Love was warm for a lifetime.
> Love grew cold in a day.
> A mermaid on the ocean
> Blew a kiss and swam away.
> Cold rain on the water
> Swelling the tide.
> Chilling the morning.
> Cold sadness inside.

"Hi," Debby said, jogging over. "Anybody see Mike running by yet?"

"Not so far, Debby," Alec smiled, "but I'll keep my eye out and try to catch him for you if he does."

Debby sat down on the blanket and crossed her legs under her, Yoga style. "Thanks, Al. But I think I can do my own catching."

"I'm sure you can, Debby," Alec laughed. "Any fish in the sea you want."

"Just remember, Debby," Felicia said. "This one's hooked."

Debby smiled. "I kind of figured that." She looked up and down the shore front for Mike. Alec figured she'd be sitting there awhile. She wasn't about to budge until she caught sight of Mike. Alec liked Debby. But he was in no mood to visit and make small talk. Not with anybody. His head was with his father even though he wasn't. And the thought of going home later and seeing his father's face after this horrible morning was almost too much to bear. Alec felt a strong urge to move every muscle in his body.

"Anybody for a swim?" he asked.

"Al," Felicia protested, "that water is cold."

"It's brisk," Alec corrected. "Good for the circulation."

"Maybe so, Al," Debby said. "But I think I'll stay here."

Alec pulled his sweatshirt over his head and took off his jeans. He left his clothes on the blanket.

"See you in a little while," he said.

"Not if I see Mike first," Debby quipped.

Alec ran quickly to the shore and plunged into the water without pausing. The shock of the cold water felt good against Alec's skin. He swam, with quick, even strokes, his mind on nothing but the sea. He swam out past the waves, then straight along the shore. After a long while he headed back toward the beach to rest. He sat down on the sand and waited a few seconds until his eyes and ears were clear of salt water.

"Al," he heard José's voice say, "I thought that drowned cat was you. How'd you get washed up on our end of the beach?"

Alec could hear the bongos now. He turned his head and saw the kids behind them a short distance up on the beach. They kept their distance. Nobody approached Alec with a word of welcome. Alec turned to face José.

"Hi, Joe," he replied. "I was just swimming. I didn't know where I landed."

"You and Columbus," José said.

"Yeah. Pull up some sand, Joe, and sit down."

José sat beside Alec at the water's edge.

"How can you swim in weather like this, Al? It's freezing in that water."

"It's cold most of the time in Russia," Alec said. "Cold never bothered me."

"I guess so. In Puerto Rico it's always warm and the water is warm too." José looked far away, as though he were dreaming of home. "Sometimes I miss it. Sometimes it feels so cold here."

"I know what you mean, Joe. You get used to the place where you grew up."

José nodded. "Yeah. This country doesn't seem like home to me." José shivered. "That wind off the ocean is strong. We're sitting near the back of the beach. Want to join us?"

"Thanks, Joe, I'd like to. But I left Felicia way on the other end of the beach."

"Sure, Al, you want to swim back to your girl. I don't blame you."

"Another time, Joe."

"Okay, Al." José waved as Alec ran toward the deep water. "Later, man," he called.

When Alec got back to his beach, he ran to Felicia and leaned down to kiss her. The book she was reading fell in the sand.

"Hey," she laughed. "Debby ran off with Mike. I thought you swam to China."

Alec sat on the blanket. "I almost did. I think I made it to Puerto Rico. I met Joe. We talked a little. I like him. He's a good guy."

"I guess so. Funny, he became top man so quickly." Felicia shrugged. "He's a good dancer, anyway."

Alec smiled. "Well, that's a step in the right direction."

Felicia winced. "Terrible joke, Al. But I don't think this whole business is a joke."

Alec nodded. "You're right. Neither do I. That reminds me. I had a run-in with Joseff on the way here."

Felicia listened as Alec told her about Joseff and the storekeeper.

"Things are getting out of hand with the street gangs, Al. The crimes are serious. I hear that in Coney Island the gangs are into robberies and muggings and stuff."

"I know. Grandpa was talking about it too. It's unbelievable."

"But it's true. I hear that the trouble between Joseff and José isn't over yet. The Russian and Puerto Rican gangs are still talking tough."

"I just don't understand it," Alec said. "If only everybody would just sit down and talk, things could be settled."

"It sounds easy," Felicia said. "But it's a lot harder than it should be."

"I know. And there are so many other troubles. We could do without troubles between the kids."

"You're right. Well, we're not fighting anyway." She leaned over and kissed him.

"That was very friendly," Alec said tenderly. He took out a cigarette and lit it. Then he held it out to Felicia, who leaned over and took a drag. Alec liked to smoke a single cigarette with Felicia. It gave a kind of closeness. A feeling that this sharing was a natural thing. A part of the sharing that would go on and on between them.

"Mom and Dad had a fight today." Felicia sighed.

"That's always rough," Alec said. "What was it about?"

"Dad was talking about buying a book store with some other people. Mom said he'll lose our last cent and we're close to it now." Felicia sighed again. "Maybe if she acted like she had more faith in him."

Alec put out the cigarette in the sand and threw the butt

into a nearby wire basket. Other people might litter the beach, but never Alec. He had a sense of order that would never leave him. Order about places and things. Order in life. And Felicia was part of that order.

"Maybe. But we never really know what goes on between people. Even our own parents. You can't really lay blame on anybody."

"It's true, Al. But sometimes I wish things were different."

"They will be, for us." He lowered Felicia slowly onto the blanket and held her close as he kissed her.

"You still feel wet," she said. "And cold."

They moved even closer, clinging together as though protecting each other against rocky ocean waves.

"You'll feel warmer in a minute," he said. "I promise."

Alec didn't feel like going home and neither did Felicia. They had a bite at Quick Grill instead of lunch or dinner.

Alec got home nearly at nightfall. When he got in, the family was sitting around the TV set quietly. You didn't have to talk to each other that way and you could avoid unpleasant topics. Nobody mentioned Papa's morning job. And Alec had the feeling that nobody ever would. It would be something Papa would keep to himself, keep inside him, one more scar that nobody could see. Alec was glad when the phone rang. Maybe now he'd hear a human voice that didn't come over the tube.

"It's for you, Papa," Alec said.

Papa rose from his chair in disbelief. Alec handed the phone to Papa, who took it as though it were a strange, newly invented instrument. Papa spoke awhile, then came back into the living room. He was actually smiling.

"That was Mrs. Kantrowitz," Papa announced. "Of the Job Opportunities Center at Beachside Y. She told me to see her personally when I came in and to make it right after the holidays. She says she thinks she might have something for me then."

"Did she say what?" Alec asked.

"No. She just said it would be something good. Something I'm really suited for. She said she would tell me about it when we meet."

Mama got up. "That's wonderful, Isaac," she said. She put her arm around Papa. He slid his arm around her waist. "That's a wonderful omen for the New Year."

"Yes," Grandpa said. "Rosh Hashanah is almost here. Next week we will be celebrating in temple."

"That's right," Mama agreed happily. "We have to get ready. There's so much to do."

Alec looked at his parents, their arms around each other, standing in the center of the living room. New Year, Alec thought. New Year in a new country. New hope and a new chance. Maybe. Just maybe.

In the coming days a lot of silverware was polished in the Steinoff household. The best old family china was taken out and washed. Closets were explored to determine what everyone would wear to temple during the holidays.

The upbeat feeling was everywhere. Neighbors smiled at each other in the hallway and greeted each other more warmly on the street. Trouble seemed to take a vacation from Brighton. To leave for a while, like birds flying south for the winter. But birds stayed away for a season. Alec doubted trouble had left this area for anywhere near that long.

Alec thought back to early spring, to the Passover seder. The Steinoffs had just come to America and it was their very first major holiday here. There were the once-a-year Passover silver and dishes. There were the seder table, set just so, with the white linens, and the matzoth, and

Grandpa reading the entire Passover Haggadah. But mostly there was hope. So much hope. Now the hope was growing tarnished, like silver nobody had polished.

Alec remembered the extra wine glass. Each Passover it was the custom for families to pour an extra glass of wine. The wine was left untouched, for the prophet Elijah who would come one Passover night, heralding the arrival of the Messiah. Well, Passover had come and was long gone, and where the hell was the Messiah? He sure was nowhere around here, where things went from bad to worse.

Yet, in spite of everything, the holiday fever was contagious. It spread to everyone, including Alec. After all, the whole family had caught it, even Papa. Mrs. Kantrowitz's call had set a mood that would last throughout the holidays. The family spent a lot of time together before the holidays. Everything had to be perfect. And Mama insisted that Natasha must have a new outfit.

"She's grown so much there's nothing for her to wear to temple that she can fit into anymore."

"I want everybody to go shopping with me," Natasha said. "We're all going to temple together and I want everybody to think I look nice."

The Steinoffs went on a shopping excursion for Natasha's new outfit. There were some other extras to look for too. Alec scanned the avenue, taking in the preholiday scene. There was really something special about this first New Year in America. Something very, very special. Grandpa said it for him.

"It is wonderful to be here!" Grandpa exclaimed. "To be getting ready for the holidays out in the open, with no fear."

"Yes," Papa said. "There was so much fear in Russia. I will never forget the raid on Papa's Talmud Torah."

Mama shook her head. "It's unbelievable when you

think about it. Raiding a Hebrew school as though it were a den of criminals."

"It's something to remember," Alec said.

"Or maybe to forget," Grandpa replied. "But forgetting is not a good idea either. Look. Look at the people buying fresh fruit for the holiday. Later on they will be buying more fruit for the holiday harvest time."

"We would have waited in line for hours in Russia," Mama said.

"Yes," Papa agreed, "for kosher food, for toothpaste, for everything."

Natasha piped up, "Remember when we were taking a walk and Grandpa stopped to tie his shoe? Everybody thought it was a line and a whole bunch of people got in back of us."

The family laughed together. "That is a funny story," Mama said. "But people really do get in any line they see. They don't know what the lines are, but they figure it must be something worth waiting for."

"That's right" Alec said. "You can't even stop to watch a sunset there without a line of people joining you."

"Yes. But here the sight of people buying kosher food gives me so much pleasure. Seeing people going to shul whenever they like gives me pleasure. It is enough for me to go to shul freely."

"It's hard to think of Grandpa as a criminal," Alec said. "But in Russia he was. Just for going to shul!"

"Except on the high holidays," Mama said. "Except on the New Year. That was the one and only time everyone broke the law."

"Yes," Grandpa recalled. "The shuls were filled. The crowds filled the temple and overflowed into the streets."

"And the authorities did nothing," Papa put in. "There were just too many people to arrest."

"There's safety in numbers," Mama said.

"A once-a-year rebellion. That's really something!" Alec exclaimed.

Natasha tugged at Alec's arm. "Look," she insisted. "Look there, down the street. A parade is coming."

Alec turned. "It does look like a parade, but I'm not sure."

Alec watched as a stream of people marched as one down the avenue. The men all wore black coats and fur hats, even in the warmth of fall. Alec recognized the clothing of the men as the garb of the Chasidim, one of the most orthodox sects of the Jewish religion.

"They are from the shul down the avenue," Grandpa said. "It is a very small shul and they worship there. This is a very special ceremony. Their shul must have gotten a new Torah for the New Year. They march through the streets with it, rejoicing, before placing it in the arc."

Traffic stopped as the crowd of people walked in the middle of the street. The chief rabbi walked in front, carrying the sacred testament in an embroidered velvet case, holding it up like a valued piece of art for all to see. It was a fantastic sight. And the joyous singing and chanting as they walked was beautiful music to hear.

"You know we would never see this in Russia," Grandpa said. "That these people can observe this ceremony in broad daylight is a marvelous thing."

"Those people are more religious than anybody, aren't they, Grandpa?" Natasha asked.

"Well, they are a very othodox sect," Grandpa answered.

"Does that mean they had a harder time in Russia?"

Grandpa thought for a moment. "No. Not really. If you were Jewish it was hard enough. Our people were oppressed and nobody asked if you were orthodox or not. As in Nazi Germany, a Jew was a Jew."

Alec looked at Natasha's blue eyes. The smiling sparkle had turned sober. Alec wondered if his sister was remembering that day in the market. That day in Russia when the little boy had taunted her, had called out "Dirty Jew." Grandpa was right. Bigotry was bigotry. In Russia, as in Nazi Germany, a Jew was a Jew.

The parade of the Chasidim was not the only outpouring of Jews that day. When the shopping excursion ended, when Natasha had her pretty new rose-colored dress, everyone went home. Alec was about to sit alone and relax with his stereo when Natasha's voice called him loudly. He got up and walked into the living room. Everyone was sitting watching Frank Winter again.

"Look at this." Natasha persisted, "Alec, you have to look."

Natasha was forever calling him to see something or other on TV. He would usually act interested for a little while and then leave the room. This time, though, Alec looked at the screen and gasped. There they were, Leonard in the lead, Misha, Betty, and the Soviet Activist Group of Beachside Y close behind, heading a long line of marchers.

"At the United Nations building," Frank Winters said, "a surprise march for Soviet Jewry. It is an orderly protest. But very impressive in number."

Alec watched as Leonard and the crowd went by, chanting and carrying posters reading

Raise the iron curtain.
Let our people go.
The children are waiting.

"We're becoming celebrities," Mama said. "Are you surprised to see your friends on TV, Alec?"

"Kind of," Alec answered. "But nothing Leonard does would really surprise me. He's one terrific guy."

"He must be," Mama said. "To have organized this march at his age."

"I'm sure he organized it," Alec said. "It's his group. I think I'll run down to the Y and see if they're back from New York. I'd love to hear what really went down."

"Let us know what you learn," Mama said.

Alec grabbed his jacket and ran down the stairs. He stopped at the sight of a stack of books, piled high in the hall outside the Karansky doorway. Mrs. Karansky was stepping around the books in order to get to her apartment. The tall, thin, dark woman stopped and turned.

"Hello, Alec," she greeted him. "I see you notice my little library."

"Yes, Mrs. Karansky," he answered. "Why are you throwing out all these books?"

"We had more room in Russia," she said sadly. "And our home. Lined with bookshelves. I just don't have enough room here. There are as many books in the apartment as I can keep. But some must go."

"Can I help carry them out for you?" Alec asked.

"Oh no, Alec. I'm leaving these in the hall. They've been here all day." She smiled. "Any neighbors are free to just stop by and take whatever they wish. They're going fast. Business has been good."

"That's a great idea, Mrs. Karansky. It's a terrific thing to do."

"You give to your neighbors," she said.

A boy about twelve years old ran up the steps. "Mrs. Karansky," he said shyly.

"Yes, son. What can I do for you?"

"Well, I took two books on Jewish history this morning. I wondered if you had any more. To study for my Bar Mitzvah."

"Of course." Mrs. Karansky pulled three books from the pile. She seemed to recognize each book without even looking at the title.

"These will help. And you come by and take any books you want. Don't be ashamed."

"Thank you, Mrs. Karansky," the boy replied. He ran down the stairs.

"Can you use any books, Alec?" Mrs. Karansky asked.

"No, thank you, Mrs. Karansky. We have lots of books in our house."

"Yes, of course. Your father and grandfather are such scholars." She sighed. "I loved our library so. It was my favorite room in the whole house. I spent hours each day there."

Mrs. Karansky's eyes were far away, as though she were looking at her house in Russia. Alec remembered Papa talking of finding Mrs. Karansky in the basement and hearing her say, "They took my home. They took my home."

"It must have been a beautiful house," Alec said.

Mrs. Karansky didn't answer Alec. She stood, surrounded by her books, looking past him. Alec walked slowly and quietly down the steps.

When Alec walked into the Y he could barely get near Leonard. A crowd of kids stood around him, asking questions.

"Best TV show I saw this year," Alec called.

Leonard laughed. "You don't watch TV, Al."

"I know, but can I join your fan club anyway?"

"Just keep helping us out when we need you."

"Sure, Leonard, but why didn't you tell me about your march? I could have helped."

"We wanted to keep it under wraps. We wanted to be sure it was a surprise, and very low-key and orderly."

"It sure was orderly."

"That was important. If you scream and yell then they holler that you're radical. The cops start busting heads. And the publicity is only sensational. This way they take you seriously. We've got to be taken seriously, Al. Everybody's got to know what's happening in Russia and about everyone locked up over there. We can't just forget about them."

"You're right and you were great. Your group is the best in the movement."

Leonard smiled. "Okay, Al. You've got the job as president of my fan club."

A hand reached right across Alec, reaching out to shake Leonard's hand. Alec ducked and moved away. "I'm leaving, Leonard," he said. "Before I get mobbed by the rest of your fan club."

Alec walked out to get some air and to wait for Felicia. He looked way up the block. By the light of the setting sun he could see two figures standing together talking on the corner.

He recognized Joseff and José. They stood still, apparently talking quietly. Then José rounded the corner and disappeared from sight. Joseff walked toward the entrance of the Y, toward Alec.

"Hi," Felicia said. "Waiting for someone or are you free?"

Alec turned. Felicia had walked from the other direction. He put his arms around her.

"Well, I've got a girl," he said. "But you're good to look at."

She laughed. "Your girl better not catch you looking," she said. "She's very jealous."

"I'll keep that in mind." Alec looked past Felicia. Joseff was walking toward the Y, not two steps away. Alec held Felicia tightly, protecting her against oncoming trouble. But Joseff just nodded, walked past them, and went quietly into the Y. First a quiet chat with José, now a peaceful stroll into Beachside without a sarcastic word. You would think Joseff had turned into a pussycat. If you didn't know better.

Alec remembered back to when he was ten years old in Russia. It was Passover, and the Sabbath. Two little boys dressed in their best clothes began fighting in the street. The mother of one of the boys opened the window.

"Stop that," she yelled loudly. "Don't you know it is Passover and Saturday?"

The boys stopped fighting and Alec heard one say to the other, "Remember after Passover and after Sabbath I'll beat you up."

That's what Joseff was doing. Calling a holiday truce. Like the little boys, waiting for the holiday to end. And Joe was going along with it. But Alec had the strong feeling that this truce was an uneasy one, uneasy and short-lived.

Alec slowly released his grip on Felicia. "Let's take a walk," he suggested. "I don't feel like being indoors right now."

"Sure. Let's walk around the block." Their path was spread with good cheer. Signs of holiday spirit were all around them. People were shopping, working in and around their houses, cleaning, repairing, and painting in readiness for the holiday season. The aroma of challah drifted from some houses, indicating that the festive holiday bread was baking inside.

"Grandpa thinks it's wonderful that the kosher butcher shops are all around us here," Alec told her. "All he has to do is walk a few blocks and ask for whatever he wants."

"That must mean a lot to your grandpa."

"You know, his Talmud Torah was raided. Teaching Hebrew and studying Hebrew are illegal in Russia. He wanted to help youngsters get ready for their Bar Mitzvahs. He had to hold classes in a darkened basement, where they had to use flashlights. Then, they raided his little class."

Felicia looked around her before she said, "It's so hard to imagine."

Alec and Felicia walked slowly down the beach block and wandered along the boardwalk. Even the boardwalk was filled with a holiday atmosphere. A crowd gathered around a man standing near the railing strumming a balalaika. He played the instrument, similar in shape and sound to a guitar, as the people around him clapped, danced, and sang Russian folk songs. An elderly couple near Felicia and Al did a spirited Russian dance with difficult steps.

"That's terrific," Felicia smiled.

"Come, dear," the man invited her. "We will dance and make your boy friend jealous."

He took Felicia's arm and she followed him to the beat of the balalaika. Alec smiled. His girl could dance in any language. The man's wife smiled to Alec as the crowd formed a circle around Felicia and her partner, clapping as they danced. Felicia bowed. "You're the best dance partner I've had in a long time," she said.

"You come dance with me anytime," the man said jovially. "Remember. A man is as young as he feels."

"Thank you. I'll remember."

Alec and Felicia smiled and walked on. They could hear the distant music of the balalaika and feel the spirit of its rhythm as they leaned against the railing and kissed in the brightness of the new moon.

The rituals of readiness for the New Year drew to a close. One of the customs was celebrated on the first day of the holiday. Felicia and Alec were walking along the board-walk. They walked over the rocks, and past the narrow bridge that led to the bay. Crowds of people stood near the railing overlooking the water. Alec saw Grandpa in the crowd. Alec and Felicia walked closer. The people were praying and chanting. Some were flinging small pieces of bread into the water, and some were just forming throw-away gestures with their hands.

"They're throwing away their sins," Felicia said. "Casting last year's sins into the water to wipe the slate clean for the New Year."

"Yes. And there's Grandpa."

"Your Grandpa." Felicia shook her head. "It's hard to figure out what sins he has."

Alec could think of a couple. But he didn't want to speak disrespectfully of his grandfather. So he just said, "I guess everybody has sins if they stop to think about it."

"Yes." Felicia spoke quietly. "I guess you and I can think of a few."

Alec looked at Felicia. He knew what she meant. But she was wrong. Alec kissed her softly. "Sure we have sins," he whispered. "But what we've got together isn't one of them. And I'm not about to throw that into the water."

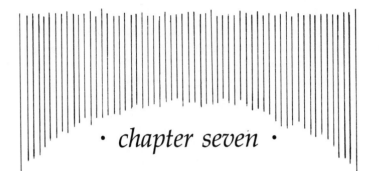

· *chapter seven* ·

The holidays were over. For a time, the warmth lingered in the chill breezes of autumn. The pictures of the temple filled with people wearing their very best clothing remained in everyone's mind. Some people wore their best clothes and smiles past the holiday, like decorations nobody could bear to take down. Like remnants of a happy time now past that no one could admit had ended.

But then the clothes went back into the closets to await another special time. The people went back to their everyday world, wearing their everyday clothes, and their strained and worried faces. Life had taken a holiday. Now it was back on the streets. Stores reopened. People returned to work. People who had no work returned to the unemployment line. Mama went to her job at JARA. Natasha went to school. And on his appointed day Papa went to the Job Opportunities Center at Beachside to see Mrs. Kantrowitz.

At dinner that night Alec thought he was in the wrong kitchen. Mama sat, tiredly picking at her food.

"I can't count the people I spoke to today," she said. "The social worker spoke about the youth problems again. She wants more funding and the money is tight. Youth problems are getting worse and so are the crimes. Crimes against people in the Coney Island area are rising."

"It's awful," Grandpa said. "Crimes against older people. The young should be learning from their elders. Instead we are all in danger."

"Don't worry," Papa soothed them. "We are in no danger here."

"Of course not, Papa," Mama said. "I don't mean to upset you. But my head is spinning from all those meetings. And most of my meetings were about the day-care center."

"What about the day-care center, Mama?" Alec asked.

"I went from one agency to another to the next. And no promise of anything definite. I don't even know who makes the final decision. I need a saw to cut through the red tape."

"But there is still hope, isn't there, Sonia?" Grandpa asked.

"I don't know, Papa. I really don't know."

Papa reached across the table and covered Mama's hand with his.

"Of course there's hope, Sonia. You must never give up. Why just when I was about to give up I heard Mrs. Kantrowitz's news."

Mama's face brightened. "You have good news, Isaac," she said excitedly. "Tell us about it."

"Well, it isn't definite. Not yet. But Mrs. Kantrowitz says the Y is planning to set up a large-scale program to teach English to Russian adults as quickly as possible. A lot of people can't find jobs because they don't know the language. And if they find jobs they can't keep them because they don't understand what's being said."

"That is a big problem," Mama said.

"Yes. And Mrs. Kantrowitz has been looking into it. She says it's a Job Opportunities problem because if people knew the language it would cut unemployment. She got a promise of government funding, and she hopes to start the program in a few weeks. She said that since I know both languages and I am a teacher, that I am just the person to head the program."

"That's great, Papa," Alec said happily.

"We must give thanks," Grandpa said.

Mama jumped up and hugged Papa. "That's wonderful, Isaac!" she exclaimed. "Can I be in your class?"

Papa laughed. "Not if you hug the teacher. It's against the rules."

"Will we be rich now?" Natasha asked seriously.

"No, honey. Teachers don't get rich. Not even the ones who set up programs. But let's not get too excited. As I told you, it is not definite."

But Papa was excited. More excited and up than Alec had ever seen him since he set foot in America. He tried to hide it, to restrain himself from counting on something not yet certain, but Alec could tell. Papa was counting on it. He had found the perfect job.

It began to look as though the Steinoffs would be back in business pretty soon. Papa would be working. Mama would probably get a better job at JARA if she swung her day-care center project. And registration and classes would begin at college in a little more than a week. Alec watched the mail every day for news about registration.

The house held an atmosphere of quiet expectation.

Things kept on an even keel for a while. Then, at last, word came from Mrs. Kantrowitz. The house of quiet expectation had been nothing more than a house of cards. And the walls were about to come tumbling down.

Papa broke the news at dinner.

"Mrs. Kantrowitz called today," he said.

"What did she say?" Mama asked.

But Mama knew the answer. All she had to do was look at Papa. His head was so low it nearly hit the kitchen table.

"It seems you have to apply very early for funding. Mrs. Kantrowitz was told she didn't get her request in on time. She can't be on the budget for this year. If she does get funds for the adult education program, it won't be until after January first."

"I know about the budget. I found that out today. I have to wait until the first of the year to reapply for the day-care center."

"You mean you have to start all over again, Mama?" Alec asked.

"I'm afraid so. But Papa's news isn't so bad." She turned to Papa. "Didn't Mrs. Kantrowitz say the job is yours when the funding comes through?"

"Yes. If the funding comes through. And that's a big if. Besides, it means another three months of waiting."

"Well," Mama laughed. "That's not very long. I waited nine months for my babies."

Papa didn't crack a smile. Mama tried one more time. "It really is encouraging. Mrs. Kantrowitz's word is good as gold. The job is yours when the funding comes through."

"Three months of waiting," Papa said. "Three more months of not knowing. And then maybe there will be no job." Papa's voice grew bitter. "Well, at least my wife is working."

"Now," Mama said. "But I am not even sure if there will be money for my job after January first. If the day-care center comes through there will be no problem though."

Alec was startled. "You mean you may lose your job, Mama?"

Mama shrugged and tossed her hair. "Who knows?" She laughed. "I don't worry. My mama used to say, 'Tomorrow takes care of itself.'" She got up and ran her hand through Papa's hair. His head was still down. "And, anyway, my husband will take care of us. I know that job will be his." She laughed.

"Come on, Isaac. Keep your chin up." She ran her hand along his cheek, bent close to him, and flirtingly tried to raise his face to meet hers, his lips to meet hers. But Papa resisted his wife's hands. He kept his head down. Down and away from her.

Alec felt himself growing angry with his father. He was taking his problems out on Mama and it wasn't fair. She was worried too, and in fear of her own job. Alec looked at his father's bent head and his anger softened. It wasn't Papa's fault. He couldn't give of himself as a man unless he felt more like a man.

Mama turned away from her husband. Alec saw her face. The cheerful, flirtatious expression was gone. Mama had been bolstering Papa amidst her own worries. She had never even spoken of her own problems. But now her face said that she was sick of being a cheerleader, sick of smiling and wearing a mask.

Nothing had improved when Alec left for the Y after dinner. He left earlier than usual and ran along the boardwalk for a while. Then he ran back along the beach block toward the Y. Felicia would be there soon and he didn't want to keep her waiting. Alec ran fast and hard.

"Hey, man," José called. "What are you running from?"

Alec slowed down. "Hi, Joe," he said. "From everything I guess."

"Yeah. But you should feel better. It's your New Year. Happy New Year, Al."

Alec smiled. Joe was okay, wishing him a happy New Year. "Thanks, Joe," he said. "But to tell you the truth the New Year isn't starting out any too great."

"What's wrong, Al?" José asked.

Alec shrugged. "Family stuff, you know."

"Yeah. That can be rough."

"Making it in a new country is rough. I don't have to tell you that, Joe."

"No. You sure don't."

"I remember when we talked at the beach one day. You told me how warm it was in Puerto Rico. How hard it is getting used to a new place. It's the same way with my folks."

"I know what you mean, Al." Joe stopped and looked out at the water. "There's this guy I knew in Puerto Rico. Manuel his name is. He came here a month or so after I did. His family moved to Manhattan."

"Did you see him in the city?" Alec asked.

Joe nodded. "I went to his house. He lived in one of those tenements. The apartment faced the back. You looked out at alleys and TV antennas on roofs."

"How did Manuel feel about that?" Alec asked.

"Well he didn't like the view. In Puerto Rico he lived in a pretty crummy shack. But he looked out on palm trees and a strip of pretty beach."

"I know how he felt," Alec said. "I sure would miss being near the water."

"So does Manuel. First time I went to see him it was daytime and the drapes were drawn. I went to open them. Manuel wouldn't let me. He said he couldn't stand to look out. You know, those drapes stay closed, day and night. Manuel still won't open them."

"That's some story, Joe," Alec said. "But I can understand it."

Alec and José walked the rest of the way together, quietly, side by side like two friends. Alec didn't say it, but it troubled him: if he and Joe could walk and talk together this way, then why couldn't the gangs?

"Are you meeting your girl?" José asked.

"At the Y," Alec answered. "I'm late now."

José stopped at the corner. "I'll hang out awhile," he said. "You have fun tonight. And hang tough."

Alec walked down the block and stood on the steps of the Y. He turned toward the corner. Joseff was approaching José, one hand in the pocket of his jeans, walking cool and slow like the hero in a bad movie. José leaned against the lamp post, standing his ground. It looked like the two leaders were about to have a talk. A very unfriendly talk. Alec remembered the quiet truce agreement before the holidays. The holidays were over now. And so was the truce. But time and trouble kept moving right ahead.

Alec walked into the Y. Nobody in the crowd was in the lounge yet. The gym was quiet. Alec walked out again and looked up and down the block. Felicia was nowhere in sight. Alec wandered to the end of the Y. He heard laughter coming from the side alley near Beachside. He walked quietly toward the sound. A group of kids sat on a ledge in the dim alley leaning against the side wall of the Y.

Ernst, Mike, and Debby sat together, and Felicia stood nearby.

"What's going on here?" Alec inquired. "A private party?"

"Kind of," Mike replied. "But you can join us."

"Well, thank you, friend," Alec said jokingly. "But what are we celebrating?"

"We're not celebrating," Mike said. "It's a little cheer-up party. We're cheering up Ernst."

Alec looked at Ernst. Even in the dimness Alec could see that Ernst was really down.

"What's wrong?" Alec asked.

"The test for the make-up classes," Ernst answered. "I flunked. Not by much. But a flop is a flop."

"That's a rotten deal, Ernst," Alec said. "I'm sorry."

"My folks wanted so much for me to be the first in the family to go to college."

"You will be. What happens now?"

"Now I have to spend another term at Hayes High. Mr. Miles was very nice when I saw him. He said it would be a small, special class for Russian students. He was sure I would graduate at the end of the term." He hit the ledge. "But back in Russia I'd be starting college by now."

"I know. But another term isn't so bad. Mr. Miles is okay. You'll graduate for sure now and you can start applying to college."

"I guess so," Ernst said, "but I feel lousy. I worked so hard."

"Yeah," Alec agreed. "You really did. But you can hang on a little longer."

"Come on, you guys," Mike said. "This is a party. We said we would cheer up Ernst and that's what we're going to do. Now I have just the thing right here." Mike reached into his pocket and pulled out a joint. "A guy in my building gave me a few. I was saving them for a good time and this is as good a time as any." Mike lit up, took a drag, and passed the joint around.

"How about you, Al?" Debby asked. "Care to join the party?"

Alec figured he could use some cheering up himself. He shrugged. "Why not? In the famous words of Morris, 'What can they do me?'"

Debby passed the joint to Alec. He took a drag and inhaled deeply. It was really good grass. It went down smooth and easy. He held the smoke in his lungs for a while, then exhaled slowly. He took one more deep drag. It didn't make him feel high, just mellow. Like all was right with the world and nothing could go wrong. The feeling only lasted for about an hour. But the way things had been going lately an hour was a long time to feel good. He held the joint out to Felicia. "How about you, honey?" he asked.

"No thanks," she said. "I'll stay with Kools."

"Whatever turns you on," Ernst said. He took the joint from Alec's hand and Alec sat in the alleyway, calm and mellow, as the sweet smell of marijuana smoke mixed with the ocean breezes and wafted through the air.

Mike had turned up with his party treat one day too soon. The next afternoon Alec looked in the mail box. The postman had brought the long-awaited word of registration. It would take place early next week as Alec had heard, and classes would begin the next day. With the registration material came news about money. And the news wasn't good.

The family sat around the kitchen table studying the material. Even city colleges charged tuition these days. Alec had applied for grants to cover the fees. Mama looked at the pile of material and shook her head.

"It's not enough," she said. "You got part of the grant, but not all."

"But what about all those papers we filled out?" Alec asked. "I nearly got writer's cramp. I thought we applied everyplace."

"We figured on federal and state aid," Mama said. "You got part of the federal grant. It's based on need. I'm working. Our income just misses being low enough to get the full amount."

Alec shook his head. "Boy, that's something else. What about the state aid?"

Papa held a paper in his hand. "This letter says that state aid goes only to people who have lived in the state for a year. We have not been here that long yet. In time we can apply. But for now, it is too soon."

Mama sat adding figures. "We really could have used that state aid," she said.

"But tuition in city colleges is very low," Alec protested.

"Yes," Mama said, "but there are extras we didn't think of."

"What kind of extras?" Papa asked.

"Well, there's a registration fee. And a student activity fee."

"That's a rip-off," Alec said angrily.

"Maybe," Mama conceded. "But it still has to be paid."

"And then there are books," Papa added. "Every course will assign different textbooks and you will have to buy them. And if you take a science course this book says you will have to pay a lab fee."

"I'll add that in too," Mama said. She sat with her column of figures, threw the pencil down hard on the table, and looked up. "No matter how I figure, it comes up minus."

"I would help if I could," Grandpa said. "But I left my pension behind when I left Russia. My income is low and I can contribute little."

Mama squeezed Grandpa's hand. "We know you would do all you could to help Alec through college. We know how you feel about education, Papa. But you just about get by yourself. We'll just have to figure out a way somehow."

"But where will the money come from?" Alec asked. "I never figured on fees and stuff."

Mama sighed; then she smiled. "Come on, Alec," she soothed him. "Didn't I tell you Grandma said that tomorrow will take care of itself? You just decide what courses you want to take and don't worry about it. We'll come up with something."

Mama's keep-smiling attempt wasn't working out too well. Even Mama couldn't keep this family smiling the way things were going. The house was heavy with gloom. There was little conversation in the family during the next few days and Alec could see there was little touching between his parents.

Mama was changing. She wore her smile less frequently. Even Natasha began looking sad. The only one not changing was Grandpa. He went about his routine, going to temple every day for morning and evening services.

Natasha was trying to cheer everybody. It was a tough job for a ten-year-old. She barged into Alec's room the night after the registration material came. Grandpa had gone to shul.

"Come on, Alec," she coaxed. "Come watch TV. Your light isn't on. And you're not even playing music."

"It's okay, little one," he said. "I'm just thinking."

"What's the matter, Alec?" she asked. "You never used to think so much."

Alec had to laugh. "I guess I'm getting old. Us old people start thinking more." He looked at Natasha. She seemed so upset.

"Don't you worry, honey," he said. "Everything will be fine. There's nothing to worry about."

Alec rumpled her hair. He knew he was lying to his kid sister, but he couldn't bear to tell her the truth. To make her grow up. Not yet. There was time for all that agony. He took her hand. "Come on, little one. Lead the way to the TV set. We'll find something to make us laugh."

Registration day drew closer. But the solution to Alec's problem remained far away. Then a few nights before registration Mama came home from work. She was late and the family was waiting dinner. Mama opened her pocketbook and wordlessly handed a small packet to Alec. Something slid from a clear plastic envelope. It was a bankbook. Alec opened to the front page and read the words "National Savings Bank. In account with Alec Steinoff."

Alec looked at the figure and gasped. "Mama, what is this?"

"This bankbook is your college account. It may not be enough to cover four years but it will go part way. I know you'll draw from it wisely and use it only for your education." Mama spoke in a clear, firm, serious, business-like tone.

"But Mama. Where did all this money come from?"

"I sold something that belonged to me. Don't concern yourself, Alec."

Mama's clear voice cracked. Alec put down the bankbook and took Mama's hands in his. Her hands were shaking uncontrollably. She tried to pull them away. That wasn't Mama. She had never drawn away from her children. Never in her life. He tightened his grip. Then he looked down and saw why she had tried to hide her hands from her son.

"Mama, your rings. Where are your rings?" Alec was afraid to hear the answer. The answer Mama had already given.

"One must do what one must do. Jewelry has gone up a lot in value since Papa bought me the engagement and wedding rings."

The diamond engagement ring and the gold wedding ring encircled with small diamonds in the same shape as the solitaire. It was a beautiful set. Mama wore both rings on the third finger of her left hand and she had never taken them off. Not ever that Alec could remember.

Papa looked up. He tried to control the shock in his voice. "Sonia. You sold your rings."

Mama kept her face to Alec. She didn't turn to Papa as she answered, "Some things are more important than others. Alec's education is more important than pretty baubles that shine in the light."

"Yes, of course, Sonia," Papa said. He kept trying to steady his tone. "You are right. That is what is important now."

"Mama," Alec began. "I don't know how to thank you. But—"

Mama didn't let Alec finish his sentence. "You don't thank your mother. You thank a stranger."

"But, Mama," Alec went on. "I can't let you do this."

"It's already done, Alec. Now forget what is past. That bankbook is for your future."

"We must get another ring," Papa said. "A plain gold one."

Mama shrugged. "A ring is only a symbol."

Alec saw the hurt in Papa's eyes. Only a symbol. Selling the rings was a symbol all right. A symbol of a marriage crumbling.

"It is a beautiful thing you have done, Sonia," Grandpa said quietly. "And my Rebecca's wedding ring is still in my drawer. I thought perhaps one day Natasha would wear it."

"I would love to wear it, Grandpa," Natasha said.

Papa smiled. Somehow, in an impossibly hopeless time for the family, it was Grandpa who had said just the right thing.

"It will be a while before you can wear it, Natasha. Now I think Papa's idea is perfect. Don't you, Sonia?"

Mama met her husband's eyes. "Yes, of course, Isaac." She turned to Grandpa. "Thank you, Papa. I would be very proud to wear Mama's ring."

Alec could barely sleep that night. Grandpa may have saved the day. But not the marriage. Since the move to America the marriage had had its ups and downs. Now the downward slide had become an avalanche. Now it began to seem that his parents had given up not only the present for their children, but the future as well.

Alec was part of the family. He had to do something. He had to help save the future. Alec was up and dressed before Grandpa went to shul. He went out onto the morning streets, walking and thinking. He had been fooling around all summer. Now it was way past time to get serious. His parents had given up so much for their children. He had to be sure their dreams for him came true. He had to make sure he got through college. He had to help.

Alec walked aimlessly down the avenue, past Knish Korner, past the clothing stores and fruit markets.

"Excuse me," he said mechanically as he bumped into someone.

"My fault," a man replied. "I didn't see you coming when I opened the door."

Alec looked up. He was standing in front of Seaview Pharmacy. The man had the swinging door opened out, and was taping a sign to the inside of the glass. Alec read

DELIVERY DRIVER NEEDED. MUST HAVE CAR.
PART TIME. SOME AFTERNOONS.
NIGHTS. SOME WEEKENDS.
APPLY WITHIN.

"Are you the owner here?" Alec asked.

"Yes. Nick Sarino." He held out his hand.

"Al Steinoff," Alec said as they shook hands. "I see you're looking for a delivery man."

"Yeah. The last one quit me last night. We want to deliver medication around Brighton after hours. I need somebody to work odd shifts and long hours. That's hard to find."

Al pulled off the taped sign and handed it to the owner. "Well, Nick," he said. "You just found someone."

Nick looked at Alec. "But you're just a kid."

"Not anymore," Alec said. "And I'm a terrific driver."

"Well. You're a big guy. And I can see you keep in shape. But you must be in school. Right? I doubt that you can handle the hours."

"Look, Nick," Alec said. "I start college next week and the money's really tight."

"But you'll need time to study. How can you manage that?"

"I'll manage. I'm a good student."

"Al, I need somebody reliable. College kids don't always show up."

"Don't worry. I'll be there when you need me."

"It's not only for me that I'm saying this. College is important. A job like this might pull your grades down. You have to think of your education."

"Nick," Alec said. "You sound like somebody's father."

Nick laughed. "I am somebody's father. My kids are young. But I'm old enough to be your big brother anyway."

"Nick, I really need the job."

Alec had to be a man, to carry his share of the work load, to help his family make it.

Nick shook Alec's hand. "Okay, Al. I'm not crazy about the idea. But the job's yours if you want it. You can start tomorrow night."

Alec got more trouble from his folks and Felicia than he had from Nick Sarino. They did nothing but hassle him about taking that job.

"You don't have to take a part-time job," Mama protested. "Not this one anyway. The hours might be too long."

"Your mother is right," Papa put in. "The job will interfere with your studies. And if you insist on working you can wait awhile. Concentrate on school at the beginning of the semester."

Felicia carried on the same way. Alec spent the next afternoon with her. It was growing cloudy and too cold to stay outdoors. Alec drove around and then parked in the brush-covered lover's lane near the bay.

"I don't like this job, Al," she said. "Afternoons and nights. Mr. Sarino didn't even tell you the hours for sure."

"I need a job, Felicia," he objected. "I have to think about the future."

Alec thought about the future each time he saw Felicia.

The future and the next generation. He and Felicia had to make good. If they failed, then the next generation didn't have a chance.

"Al," she insisted, "this job is not your future."

Alec didn't feel like arguing. Instead he eased Felicia down on the car seat and covered her mouth and body with his.

After a long while, Felicia sat up, straightened her clothes, and combed her hair. She leaned her head against her boy friend's shoulder.

"Al," she said. "I still don't like it."

"No kidding? I liked it fine. What did I do wrong?"

She slapped his chest playfully. "Oh. You know what I mean." Her voice grew worried. "I don't like the idea of your taking that job."

"Will you quit worrying, baby?" He kissed her and she clung to him tightly. "If you don't watch it you'll be worrying about me for the next hundred years."

At dinner the next night Papa barely spoke. He toyed with his food and looked down into his plate instead of at his family. At last he raised his eyes.

"Alec," he asked, "are you using the car tonight?"

"If it's okay with you, Papa. I'm delivering for Mr. Sarino. I leave pretty soon."

"Well, then can you drive me to work? And call for me later?"

Mama spoke up excitedly. "You got the job, Isaac? Did Mrs. Kantrowitz call you?"

"No," Papa answered. "I'll have to wait at least three months. And Alec needs help with his college expenses now. I called the Professional Office in Manhattan."

"You don't mean that creep that got you the messenger job."

"I spoke with that interviewer. Yes."

"Boy. What did he say now?"

"He had a job offer in a business nearby. It's just temporary. He needed someone to help serve at Creamy Custard."

"Papa, that's ridiculous."

"No, Isaac, that is not for you," Mama objected. "Working at a custard stand in Brighton!"

"It is not the one in Brighton," Papa said calmly. "It is a different Creamy Custard on Surf Avenue."

"Coney Island!" Alec exclaimed. "Papa, you can't work there at night. It's rough over there. Who's working with you?"

Papa shrugged. "Maybe one other person. Maybe just me."

"You just can't work alone," Alec insisted.

Grandpa nodded. "Listen to Alec. You cannot go."

Mama frowned and shook her head. "They are right, Isaac. I don't like the stories I hear about the gangs in that neighborhood." She took Papa's hand. "Mrs. Kantrowitz's funding will come through," she said soothingly. "You'll see." Her voice grew soft and coaxing. "You'll see that everything will work out. Now just forget about this and keep me company tonight."

Papa softened but he did not melt. He pressed his wife's hand. "Thank you for worrying, Sonia. But there's nothing to worry about. I will be fine. And this is just temporary. Just to earn a little money for Alec's education. Just until the adult education program is funded."

After dinner the family gave it one more try. But Papa wouldn't budge. He was determined to earn some money for Alec's college tuition. Mama saw that it was no use. She sighed and looked out the window.

"It's drizzling," she observed. She took Papa's raincoat from the closet and held it for him as he slipped into it. "Take care of him, Alec," she said.

"I'll try, Mama," Alec answered. Alec opened the door.

Mama hugged Papa for a moment and kissed him. "Take care," she said softly.

Alec dropped Papa at Creamy Custard.

It was still light and the Coney Island streets were filled with people. Crowds stood in front of Nathan's and music blared from honky-tonks as Alec headed to Seaview Pharmacy to pick up his work.

By the time Alec finished his deliveries he was shivering. He walked down the avenue, the collar of his denim jacket up. A chill wind was blowing off the water and a cold autumn drizzle was turning into rain. A hard rain had begun to fall when Alec got into the car and headed back to pick up Papa.

Alec switched on the wipers and the radio. He caught the last verse of the Native Son hit.

> Ocean waves, keep on rolling.
> Morning sunrise, warm the shore.
> New lovers, build sand castles.
> Sun shines for me no more.
> Cold rain on the water
> Swelling the tide.
> Chilling the morning.
> Cold sadness inside.
> We walk on the wet sand
> Sea birds and me.
> Cold rain on the water.
> Cold rain on the sea.

Alec drummed the rhythm on the steering wheel with one hand and looked down the beach block toward the ocean. That sure was an appropriate tune for tonight. A cold rain was falling on the water and the night was overcast and raw. Alec drove down Surf Avenue to Coney

Island. He pulled up and stopped near Creamy Custard. He parked and walked out onto the darkened, deserted, rain-slicked sidewalk.

Then Alec heard the scuffling sounds. Through the darkness he could see the shadowy figures running toward him. Through the darkness he could see the silvery glint of the knife blade. "Go, man, go. Go, man, go," a kid said impatiently. "Go, man, go." The rhythm of those words echoed through Alec's mind like a distant long-forgotten drum beat. Then it came back to him. The same rhythm, the same chorus, as back in Russia. "Go, Jew, go. Go, Jew, go. Go, Jew, go."

Alec stood on the curb beside his car. He tried to accustom his eyes to the darkness, to see faces. The voices told him the kids were Spanish. For one panicky moment he looked around for Joe. Joe was his friend. He would protect him. But this was another gang, another turf, another world. There was no Joe anywhere around. The kids raced past him, into the gutter, across the street and out of sight. Alec ran to the open doorway of Creamy Custard and gasped. Only then did Alec realize what the kids had been running from.

"Papa!" Alec cried. "Papa. Get up."

But Papa didn't move. He lay on his side, one arm outstretched as though he had crawled toward the door, hoping to make it to the street, to help. The door was open and Papa lay, half in and half out of the entranceway, unable to crawl any farther. Alec watched in horror as his father's blood trickled out onto the streets of their new land.

Alec sat on the wet, bloody pavement and gently lifted Papa's face onto his lap. He sat, crying uncontrollably, cradling his father's head.

"Papa," he said again and again. "Papa, get up. Papa, please get up."

Then Alec's voice grew quiet. Papa could not get up. Not ever again. He had come to this country for his children. He had given so much for his children. And now he had given his life.

Sirens sounded, grew louder, then stopped, and Alec could see the reflection of flashing red lights on the wet pavement. Policemen stood over Alec and Papa, bending near, speaking quietly.

"He pressed the silent alarm," one policeman said. "But we're too late. Robbery and murder now."

"His wallet's gone. No identification. Call the owner for his name so we can notify his family."

"Isaac Steinoff," Alec heard himself saying. "I'm his son, Al. And I'll go home and tell my folks myself." Alec's voice broke. "I'll go home soon."

Alec pressed his lips to his father's cheek. He hugged Papa tightly. Then he felt a hand squeezing his shoulder. "Come, Al," a policeman said gently. "There's nothing more you can do for your father now."

Alec remembered Papa's words the night the family had decided to leave Russia. "Each generation makes the next one better." Papa had done all he could. Now the future was out of Papa's hands. Now it was Alec's time. Alec looked at his father, then at the policeman.

"I can try, officer," he answered softly. "I can sure try."